"This lighthearted peek into small-town secrets and rumors carries enough good humor, emotional honesty, plot twists, and recipes to entertain and satisfy."
—*Publishers Weekly*

"A delightful amateur sleuth that is not only exciting but also never melts down." —*Midwest Book Review*

"Watson takes the mystery reader on a wild Texas stampede in *I Scream, You Scream.* . . . Humor abounds and the novel features lively, interesting characters."
Gumshoe

"*I Scream, You Scream* is just plain fun to read, with great characters and wonderful sensory detail . . . that makes people and places come alive. . . . Needless to say, it's easy for me to recommend *I Scream, You Scream* to the pickiest of cozy readers." —Cozy Library

OTHER BOOKS IN THE
MYSTERY À LA MODE SERIES
BY WENDY LYN WATSON

*I Scream, You Scream*
*Scoop to Kill*

# A Parfait Murder

## A Mystery à la Mode

*Wendy Lyn Watson*

AN OBSIDIAN MYSTERY

OBSIDIAN
Published by New American Library, a division of
Penguin Group (USA) Inc., 375 Hudson Street,
New York, New York 10014, USA
Penguin Group (Canada), 90 Eglinton Avenue East, Suite 700, Toronto,
Ontario M4P 2Y3, Canada (a division of Pearson Penguin Canada Inc.)
Penguin Books Ltd., 80 Strand, London WC2R 0RL, England
Penguin Ireland, 25 St. Stephen's Green, Dublin 2,
Ireland (a division of Penguin Books Ltd.)
Penguin Group (Australia), 250 Camberwell Road, Camberwell, Victoria 3124,
Australia (a division of Pearson Australia Group Pty. Ltd.)
Penguin Books India Pvt. Ltd., 11 Community Centre, Panchsheel Park,
New Delhi - 10 017, India
Penguin Group (NZ), 67 Apollo Drive, Rosedale, Auckland 0632,
New Zealand (a division of Pearson New Zealand Ltd.)
Penguin Books (South Africa) (Pty.) Ltd., 24 Sturdee Avenue,
Rosebank, Johannesburg 2196, South Africa

Penguin Books Ltd., Registered Offices:
80 Strand, London WC2R 0RL, England

First published by Obsidian, an imprint of New American Library,
a division of Penguin Group (USA) Inc.

First Printing, June 2011
The song lyrics on page 197 are from Dan Hill's "Can't We Try."
Excerpt from *I Scream, You Scream* copyright © Wendy Watson, 2009
10  9  8  7  6  5  4  3  2  1

Copyright © Wendy Watson, 2011
All rights reserved

*Six Peter, Always*

# Acknowledgments

It took a village to write this book, and any effort to identify all the folks who helped would surely miss someone. Three people deserve special mention, however. First, the incredible artist who has worked on my covers has made my heart go zing with every one. Second, my agent, Kim Lionetti, has been a dogged cheerleader, both of the Mysteries à la Mode and my career more generally; I cannot thank her enough. Finally, for this book in particular, my editor, Sandy Harding, has been an enormous help. Not only was she patient with my stuttering start, but she provided some great suggestions for making the final product infinitely better.

As always, I couldn't write a word without the love and support of my husband. Thank you, baby, for cleaning the cat box and making dinner and quietly playing computer games on all those days I huddled deep in the writing cave. I love you.

# *chapter 1*

Eloise Carberry folded her arms across her pink-aproned bosom, *tsk*ed softly, and shook her head as she threw down the figurative gauntlet. "They sure look alike to me."

Tucker Gentry drew himself up straight and tight as a banjo string. "Criminy, Eloise. It's ice cream. It all pretty much looks the same."

She *tsk*ed again.

Tucker and Eloise squared off over a stainless steel table, bare save for two white paper cups, each holding a single melting scoop of ice cream. One of those cups contained Tucker's entry in the hand-churned ice cream category of the Lantana County Fair, a flavor he called "pepper praline." The other cup held a scoop of Texas Twister from Remember the A-la-mode, a smooth vanilla with a swirl of dulce de leche and a kick of ancho chilies.

"They don't just look the same. They taste the same," Eloise insisted. Her claim drew gasps from the crowd behind her. Word of the scandal must have spread through the fairgrounds, as the gathering in the creative arts exhibit pole barn was growing by the minute.

Tucker was just a little fella, his shoulder blades clearly visible beneath the wash-worn cotton of his blue plaid shirt, but he had honed his speaking voice through years as the youth pastor at the One Word Bible Church. "I assure you, if Tally's ice cream and mine taste the same, it's not my doing."

Every head in the crowd swiveled in unison to look at me.

As one of the judges in the edibles division, I had been in the exhibit when Eloise made her charge against her fellow competitor, but since it was my own recipe Tucker had allegedly copied, I'd quickly recused myself from taking any part in resolving the matter. Still, I didn't consider the dispute personal until Tucker turned the tables and implied *I* was the thief.

Under the scrutiny of all those onlookers, I felt the burn of a blush lick up my cheeks.

I was still trying to figure out how to respond to Tucker's veiled accusation when my grandma Peachy elbowed her way in front of me.

"Young man," she barked, "you mess with my girl, you mess with me."

Some folks might not think an eighty-five-year-old woman with a bum knee would be much of a threat. But Peachy's name is the only sweet thing about her. She can shoot as straight as she can spit, and I've seen her stand down a longhorn bull with nothing but a wire whisk in her hand.

If Tucker Gentry'd had the good sense God gave little bunny rabbits, he'd have tucked his tail between his legs and apologized. But instead he narrowed his eyes as if he were going to go toe-to-toe with Peachy.

Garrett Simms cleared his throat. He stood a head taller than anyone else in the room, had to be close to six-four, with pale red hair all over his head and just about every visible bit of skin. Despite his height and hirsuteness, he had gentle features, womanly hips, and a quiet, lilting voice. Normally, Garrett didn't command much respect. But as the head judge of the edibles division of the Lantana County Fair, he wielded considerable power. When he held up his soft, pale hands in a plea for silence, the bickering stopped.

"Miss Ver Steeg and I will decide whether Mr. Gentry's entry should be disqualified."

Kristen Ver Steeg, the third judge on the panel, shook her head. "Sorry, Garrett. I need to recuse myself, too."

I can't speak for the whole crowd, but Kristen's announcement caught me off guard. Kristen Ver Steeg was a relative newcomer to Dalliance, having opened a small law firm in town just a few years before. Both her office and her swank condo community were out on FM 410, in the part of Dalliance that was more suburb than small town. The only reason she'd been given a spot on the judging panel was that, as a former member of the pageant circuit, she'd volunteered to coordinate the Lantana Round-Up Rodeo Queen Pageant.

In short, Kristen was a Dalliance dilettante. I couldn't imagine she'd ever crossed paths with Tucker Gentry. And while she might know Eloise Carberry—as the reigning president of the League of Methodist Ladies and a founding member of the Dalliance Fat Quarters quilting club, Eloise knew just about everybody—the two women couldn't have enough history to justify Kristen recusing herself. After all, Dalliance is the sort of town where you can't sneeze without someone's second cousin saying "God bless"; we had to play fast and loose with notions of "bias" if we wanted to put together a panel of judges for any of the fair competitions.

Garrett Simms must have shared my surprise. "Really?" he asked.

By way of an answer, Kristen moved a step away from the table.

Garrett shrugged. "All right, then. I guess I'll make the call."

Eloise Carberry handed him a plastic spoon, and Garrett picked up the first cup of ice cream. Tucker's.

Garrett had just closed his fleshy pink lips around the spoon when my cell phone started vibrating in the front pocket of my jeans.

I pulled it out, cussing under my breath. The screen indicated it was my cousin Bree calling. She was manning the A-la-mode booth over on the midway.

I hustled a few yards away, ducking behind a shelving unit lined with jars of preserves, and answered.

"What's up?"

"Hey," Bree said. She never moved faster than a sashay, but she sounded as if she'd been running. "I need you back here, pronto. You and Peachy. And bring that man of yours, too."

"Is everything okay? Is Alice all right?" About the only thing Bree got worked up about was her precocious teenage daughter. Alice didn't raise much heck, but she still managed to get herself into some sticky situations.

"She's fine as frog's hair. For now."

"Well, I'm kinda busy here," I said. "Eloise accused Tucker of stealing an A-la-mode recipe—"

"Tally," Bree snapped. "This is an emergency. You'll never in a million years guess who just moseyed past the booth."

"Who?"

"Sonny Anders."

"No." The last anyone had seen of Alice's daddy, he'd kissed his toddler child on the forehead before driving off into the night with an exotic dancer named Spumanti.

"Yep. Just strutting down the midway, bold as brass."

"Sweet Jesus," I breathed.

Bree laughed. "I don't think the good Lord had anything to do with this."

Garrett was still contemplating the two dishes of ice cream, lifting first one spoon to his lips, then the other, his freckled brow crumpled up like a used dish towel.

Quietly as I could, I told Kristen Ver Steeg I had to go. "Family emergency," I explained. The corners of her mouth tightened a smidge, but she didn't show any other sign of interest or concern.

I took Peachy by the hand and skedaddled out of there. As we ducked out of the barn, I glanced over my shoulder. I could see Garrett speaking, his hands clasped behind his back. Garrett's large frame blocked my view of Tucker Gentry, but I didn't need to see his grin to know what Garrett had decided. Eloise Carberry's face had gone as pink as her apron, and as Garrett spoke she shook her head like a terrier with a chew toy. I felt bad that Garrett had to deal with Eloise on his own—Kristen had distanced herself from the ice cream debate and had her cell phone plastered to her ear, and I couldn't stick around to help smooth the waters—but if anyone could restore peace, Garrett was the man.

Peachy and I made our way to the Remember the A-la-mode booth on the fair's midway as quickly as Peachy's arthritis would allow. As we hustled across the dusty fairgrounds, I called Finn Harper on my cell phone and asked him to poke around a bit about Sonny's sudden appearance and then meet us back at the booth.

Finn and I had dated in high school, our relationship burning with that peculiar passion that seems reserved for adolescents. A week before we graduated, I dumped him in the Tasty-Swirl parking lot. He roared into the night in his dark green Sirocco, and I didn't see hide nor hair of him for the next seventeen years.

Then one day he literally turned up on my doorstep, all grown up and looking more sinful than a double-dip hot fudge sundae with extra whipped cream, and pretty soon he was helping me solve a murder. We'd spent a few months dancing around each other, nervous as pigs at a barbecue, trying to figure out which feelings were real and which were the ghosts of a love long gone, before we began dating for real.

Finn wasn't just pretty to look at. He had a good head on his shoulders, and his position as a reporter for the *Dalliance News-Letter* meant he had access to all kinds of information. If anyone could ferret out why Sonny Anders had slithered back to town, Finn could.

Peachy and I made our way along the stretch of the fairgrounds devoted to food stalls, past the standard fair fixtures—corn dogs, fried Twinkies, and funnel cakes—and the local favorites like the Bar None's beer booth and El Guapo's taco stand. It was only the first day of the fair and not quite noon, so attendance hadn't picked up yet. The workers were still enjoying the peace as they prepped their booths for the crush of the first evening, and several shouted out friendly hellos as we passed.

We found Bree pacing the twenty-foot length of the A-la-mode booth, back and forth like a tin duck in a shooting gallery. She braced one arm across her belly while she chewed on the thumbnail of the other hand.

"What took you so long?" she snapped.

I jerked my head subtly toward Peachy. When my grandma looked in the mirror, I fancy she still saw herself with a full head of auburn curls and bright eyes that could lure a man to her bedroom or knock him flat on his backside, depending on her mood. She did not care to be reminded of her infirmities. "It's a long hike," I hedged.

"Well, I about piddled myself when I saw Sonny, walking down the midway without a care in the world. Like it was no big deal to just show up in Dalliance after fifteen years." Bree plopped down on one of the folding chairs we'd set up for slow times, and Peachy gingerly lowered herself into the other.

"Did you say something? Did he see you?" I asked.

Bree laughed. "I don't think he saw me, and I was too stunned to speak. Lord, what am I gonna tell Alice?"

"You'll tell her the truth," Peachy said. "That girl's got more sense than the two of you put together. She's not gonna have a conniption just because her daddy's back in town."

"He looked good."

Peachy sucked her teeth, her lip curled in contempt. "Now, you just keep those hormones holstered, little girl."

Bree rolled her eyes dramatically. "Not that kind of good, Gram. Give me a little credit. I mean he looks like he's doing good. Wearing a suit and everything. I almost didn't recognize him. And he was walking with a woman on his arm."

"A wife?" I asked.

Bree looked as if she'd smelled something funky. "Maybe. But for all I know, Sonny thinks we're still married."

When Sonny split town, he didn't leave a forwarding address. Bree had to jump through a million and one hoops—and wait over a year—to serve process through newspaper publication and obtain a divorce on the grounds of abandonment.

She shrugged. "Whoever she was, she was a fair step up from that skank Spumanti. Lord, do you remember her?" Bree shivered dramatically. "That was the most humiliating part of Sonny leaving, the fact that he left me for that sorry creature."

Spumanti had been a dancer out at the Pole Cat, famous for its cheap ribs and cheaper girls. I only saw her a couple of times, when Bree dragged me along to hear Sonny's band play crappy Skynyrd covers before the dancers took the stage.

None of the girls at the Pole Cat were much to look at. If a dancer had a good body and a few moves—and wasn't suffering from meth-mouth—she could make a lot more cash at one of the clubs off Harry Hines in Dallas or in the rougher clubs over in Fort Worth. In fact, the Pole Cat got a lot of runoff from those more upscale establishments. Girls who got fired for getting too close to the customers or doing drugs at work would show up at the Pole Cat, and the Pole Cat let everything with two X chromosomes work the pole.

But even for the Pole Cat, Spumanti was sorta pitiful. Something about her—her lank blond hair, her unwholesome complexion, her lifeless eyes—something reminded me of overcooked grits.

"Dang," I said, smothering a snort of laughter, "you remember that tattoo of hers?"

Peachy perked up. "What tattoo?"

"She had this upended champagne bottle on her

tummy, made it look like someone was pouring champagne on her . . . well, you know."

Peachy whistled. "Her mama must have been so proud."

"I don't think her mama cared a lick," Bree said. "Which is how she ended up stripping and running off with a married man. Anyway, I bet this new lady doesn't have a tattoo on her cooch. She was dressed all classy, like a Junior Leaguer."

"Are you sure she was with Sonny?" I quipped.

Bree snorted. "Sonny always did like a little sin in his sugar." Her lips twisted in a self-deprecating smile. My cousin had a big ol' brain and a heart the size of Texas, but she also had a wild streak a mile wide. Even dressed for scooping ice cream, in a skintight Remember the A-la-mode T-shirt and sprayed-on skinny jeans, she looked like trouble. Norma Jean Baker just waiting to be transformed into Marilyn.

She shrugged. "The lady was a little buttoned up for Sonny, but she had a wiggle in her walk. And maybe his tastes have matured a bit."

Peachy dipped a hand in the wide pocket of her barn jacket, which she wore no matter the occasion or the weather, and pulled out her pipe and a rolled bag of tobacco. With fingers gnarled by age but still sure and steady, she set about the small ritual of filling her bowl with her favorite dark cherry blend.

"Gram," I said, "you can't smoke in here."

She shot me the hairy eyeball. "Says who?"

"Says the government. It's a fire hazard and probably a health hazard, too."

She snorted. "This pipe's safer than that old rattle-trap ice cream freezer."

We all paused to study the freezer. It was a bit disreputable, its motor emitting a high-pitched whine as it struggled to fight against the brutal August heat.

"That may be," I conceded, "but the law doesn't see it that way."

"Lord a'mighty," she said, even as she began rerolling her tobacco stash. "You're no better than the clipboard Nazis out at Tarleton Ranch."

Peachy had recently given up the real ranch she'd managed for the last fifty-some years in favor of a studio apartment—complete with all the amenities of modern life—at a senior living community called Tarleton Ranch. She joked that the only livestock at Tarleton Ranch were blue-haired hens and randy old goats.

Peachy carped about the rules (especially the one that made her go outside to smoke her pipe), the food, the "clipboard Nazis"—who were really just aides who patrolled the halls checking on the residents, and even the upholstery in the card room, but that was just Peachy's way. She wouldn't stop finding fault until she cocked up her toes for good. I could tell that, deep down, she was having a blast bossing around the other ladies and flirting with the gents.

"Hello?" Bree waved her hand above her head trying to get our attention. "Can we get back to my problem?"

I pulled a can of diet soda from a chest cooler and then sat on the lid as I cracked it open. "I know it's a shock, Bree, but I'm not really sure it's a 'problem.'"

"Heck yes, it is. We have to keep him away from Alice. That man isn't getting within a hundred yards of my child."

Peachy harrumphed. "Alice can decide for herself if she wants to see her daddy. And whatever she decides, we support her." Bree opened her mouth to argue, but Peachy cut her off with a waggle of her finger. "It's her choice, Sabrina Marie. Not yours."

Before they could get into a knock-down, drag-out fight, Finn poked his head over the counter of our stall. "Hey. Can I come in?"

Every time I saw the man, my heart went pitter-pat. I gave him a big dopey smile and gestured to the door on the side of the stall. He smiled back before he disappeared, a little heat and promise in his evergreen eyes.

"So I asked around," he said when he'd joined us inside. "Didn't take long for the word to get around. Sonny's not exactly lying low."

"What's he doing here? Where the heck has he been?" Bree demanded.

Finn held up his hands in a placating gesture. "I'm going as fast as I can, Bree."

I handed him a soda and he leaned his back against the wall, settling in for a good chat. "Okay, so I don't know how long Sonny was up north, but he apparently spent some time in Pennsylvania developing a natural gas field there."

"Natural gas?" I said.

Bree snorted. "The only way Sonny could develop gas is to eat a can of beans."

"Wow," Finn said. "Aren't you just the picture of genteel southern womanhood? I can't believe the League of Methodist Ladies hasn't recruited you for their board."

She flipped him the finger, and he laughed.

"Look, I'm just telling you what I heard. Dave Epler from the Chamber of Commerce said Sonny showed up at the Parlay Inn last night, buying rounds of ten-buck-a-glass Scotch, and talking about how he made a bundle working an old field with some hot new technology. He's got the wad of bills and the shiny sports car to prove it."

"Who's the woman?" Bree asked. The chill in her voice made me shiver despite the triple-digit weather.

"That I don't know," Finn admitted.

"And why's he here?"

Finn shrugged. "Dave said Sonny got real cagey when folks started asking him that. But Dave and Mike Carberry got to talking, and they think maybe Sonny has a bead on a way to extract more gas from the Altemont Shale."

The Altemont Shale was a geologic formation that ran under dang near all of Lantana County. Petroleum soaked the rich, porous rock, but getting it out had never been cost-effective. New developments in drilling technology, though, had made other similar shale deposits profitable, and so squeezing black gold from the Altemont had become a favorite source of speculation for the barflies and old-timers around town.

Bree snorted. "All I know is if Sonny Anders has money, he owes me a passel of it."

Finn raised a questioning eyebrow.

"Sonny never paid a lick of child support," I explained.

"That should be easy to fix. The state should be able to calculate what he owes based on the order and go after him for it. You don't need to lift a finger."

"There is no order," I said.

Bree'd been taken to task for her failure to secure a support order often enough to anticipate Finn's reaction. "Before you go off on me, just remember that when Sonny left, he hadn't had a paying job in over a year."

"No-good, shiftless piece of garbage," Peachy snarled.

"Yes'm, I know," Bree sighed. "Huge mistake marrying him. But spilt milk and all that. Anyway, far as I knew, getting child support from Sonny would be like getting blood from a turnip. Probably would have cost me more to find him and sue him than I ever would have got out of the deal. And I had a baby girl to raise all on my own. I didn't have the money to spend hunting down that sleazeball."

"Is it too late?" Finn asked.

"Nope," Bree said. "Alice is still a minor, won't be eighteen until next February."

Finn frowned and I could see the wheels turning behind his eyes. I was just about to ask him what was on his mind when Peachy spat—loudly—on the ground at my feet.

"Speak of the devil and he shall appear," she growled.

In unison, Bree, Finn, and I turned to follow Peachy's slit-eyed stare. There, leaning over the counter with a big ol' grin on his face, stood Sonny Anders.

# chapter 2

Sonny'd aged a fair piece, and he'd definitely changed his look. When Bree and Sonny were an item, he'd been channeling his inner Elvis with a rockabilly pompadour, tight T-shirts, and a permanent sneer. That afternoon at the fair, he looked like a business tycoon of the old-school Texas variety: short, slicked hair, three-piece suit, and a bolo tie.

Still, Bree lied when she said she almost didn't recognize him. I'd have known him anywhere. He'd always been whip thin and sinewy, as tough and spare as the west Texas desert he called home. If he'd put on a paunch, I couldn't see it beneath his snazzy suit vest. A bit of silver threaded through his coal black hair, but it hadn't thinned or receded a bit. Sleepy lids fringed with ridiculously long lashes hooded his near-black eyes, making him look as if he'd just roused after a night of wickedness. He had a few more lines on his face—the mark of a man who'd spent his youth in the unforgiving Texas sun—but otherwise, he just looked like Sonny.

In other words, like the devil himself.

"Hey, y'all," he said, honey dripping from every syllable, "I heard this is the place to get something cool and creamy."

Bree shot out of her seat and lunged across the counter. Finn and I both grabbed for her, struggling to pull her away, while Sonny danced back, his hands raised in surrender.

"Sabrina Marie," Peachy barked, "cool your jets."

Bree relaxed in my grasp, but her eyes still burned with pure hate.

Sonny eyed the neatly printed sign propped next to the samples of our signature salted caramel sauce: CARAMEL KNOWLEDGE: TRY SOME!

"Don't mind if I do," he murmured. He picked up a tiny clear plastic cup with a lime green tasting spoon propped in a puddle of gooey amber deliciousness. He managed to get the spoon to his mouth before a drip of caramel escaped, closed his lips around the treat, and moaned. "Oh my. Sin on a spoon."

"Have a little more, Sonny," Bree growled. "Maybe we can send you straight to hell."

Sonny's eyes narrowed and he chuckled softly. "I missed you, too, kitten," he purred.

"Jackass," Bree snapped.

He *tsk*ed. "Is that any way to greet an old friend?"

"You are no friend of mine, Sonny Anders. Friends

don't take off in the middle of the night without so much as a note."

Sonny cocked an eyebrow. "Technically it was the middle of the afternoon. But I see your point."

"Uh-huh. You'll be seeing my point in court, mister," Bree said. As zingers went, it fell a little flat, but she was way too p.o.'d to come up with a snappy retort. "I hear you finally stopped mooching off of women and got yourself a job. Maybe it's about time you took care of your child, don't you think?"

A shadow flickered over Sonny's face. For a second I thought I'd witnessed a miracle: real human emotion from Sonny Anders, some warmth beneath the facade of reptilian charm. But then the shadow passed and he grinned.

"I'm one step ahead of you, kitten, and I couldn't agree more." He rocked back on his heels and tucked the tips of his fingers in his pants pockets. "I've enjoyed a certain material success in the last few years, and I would be honored to share that bounty with the fruit of my loins."

Bree frowned, and I felt a twinge of unease in the pit of my gut. This seemed too easy.

Way too easy.

"Yessir," Sonny continued, his voice rich and well modulated, like an old-time Dixiecrat making a stump speech on election day, "I will support my child. Assuming she is my child."

Bree snapped to attention, and I tightened my hold on her arm. "What are you implying?" she growled.

"I'm not implying anything, kitten. Just doing my due diligence, like any good businessman would."

Peachy shouldered her way past me, Finn, and Bree, to square off against Sonny over the counter of our booth.

"Listen up, young man. You deny that precious grand-child of mine and I will personally see to it that you get a sneak peek at hell before you die. You got that?"

Sonny laughed. "Jeez, kitten, I see where you get your claws." He tutted softly, as if he were calming an ornery animal. "I'm not denying nothin'," he said. "I'm just gonna let science make the call."

He glanced to his left and his smile brightened. "I'll just let the counselor here explain."

We all followed his line of sight. Kristen Ver Steeg headed our way. The blistering sun washed the color from her pale lemon suit and her champagne-colored upswept hair. With her face devoid of expression, she looked as if she were carved out of butter.

A big man all in black—jeans, T-shirt, leather vest, biker boots, and wraparound shades—followed close behind her. He looked vaguely familiar, but it took a moment for me to place him.

Nick DeWinter, better known as "Neck," graduated a year behind me in high school. He was a star defensive lineman until he got caught boosting car stereos in the teacher parking lot. I'd heard he did a little time after school, but that might have just been gossip. Still, he looked as if he could go toe-to-toe with the baddest felon in the yard.

His dark massiveness made slim, pale Kristen look even more fey by comparison.

The unlikely duo marched up to the booth.

Kristen offered us a bland smile and extended her hand toward Bree. Bree glanced at the proffered hand but did not take it. Kristen's smile tightened, but never wavered as she let her hand drop to her side.

"Ms. Michaels, my name is Kristen Ver Steeg. Mr. Anders has retained me to represent him in regards to his paternity suit."

Bree, Finn, Peachy, and I all spoke at once. "Paternity suit?"

Kristen cleared her throat. Her eyes darted briefly in Sonny's direction. "Yes. I would urge you to retain a lawyer, but I think you'll find the complaint self-explanatory."

She looked at Neck and jerked her head toward Bree. Neck stepped forward and reached a hand around his back to pull something from his waistband. I was halfway into a crouch, expecting a gun, before I realized he held nothing more deadly than an envelope.

He stretched his arm across the counter and waved the envelope. "Bree Michaels?" he asked in a voice that sounded like gravel at the bottom of a well.

"Uh-huh," Bree choked, a trembling hand taking the envelope from his fingers.

"You've been served."

# *chapter 3*

In the end, it might have been easier for Bree if Neck had pulled a gun out of his pants. At least doctors can remove bullets.

Kristen, Neck, and Sonny took off right after serving Bree with the papers claiming Sonny wasn't Alice's father. We were left to clean up the mess.

Bree sagged into the folding chair, her hands trembling as she unfolded the paper, her eyes haunted as they scanned the words written there.

"Son of a . . ." She threw the packet of papers across the booth. "He's claiming I was a tramp."

Finn bent down to scoop them up. "I'm sure it doesn't say that," he muttered, handing the papers back to Bree.

"Not in so many words, but that's the gist. This paragraph right here"—she stabbed at the paper as if

she were squashing the life out of the printed words—
"says 'Plaintiff is informed and believes and based
thereon alleges the Defendant engaged in an ongoing
and public course of sexually promiscuous behavior
during the months prior and subsequent to June of
1992, including but not limited to the evening of June
twenty-second, 1992.'" She made a choking sound. "And,
of course, he points out that Alice was born less than
nine months after he and I met."

Finn cocked his head, his eyebrows wrinkling into a
look of shock. "What?"

Bree speared him with a hard stare. "It's not what
you think," she said, each word a tight little packet of
pain. "Alice was premature. Her due date was nine
months to the day after Sonny and I first . . . met." She
sniffed and lifted her chin. "We hooked up at a party
to mark the start of summer." A hard laugh escaped
her. She waved the papers in her hand, and scrunched
up her face in mock seriousness. "'On or about June
twenty-second,'" she intoned. Then the starch went out
of her spine. "Alice was due on March fifteenth, but
she was born on Valentine's Day."

She dropped her chin and stared at her hands, resting limp in her lap. "She was so tiny. My little peanut."

"Hey, Mom! Aunt Tally!"

My heart leaped into my throat at Alice's excited
shout. She tumbled into the tiny booth with Kyle Mason, my employee and Alice's boyfriend, practically
on top of her. She looked around at the crowd of solemn faces and giggled. "Look, Kyle, it's everybody!"

Kyle folded his lanky body around my little slip of

a niece, his arms encircling her. If he could have cradled her in bubble wrap, he would have.

They were an unlikely pair. Kyle had finally won a war of attrition with his high school teachers and graduated in June, while my precocious seventeen-year-old niece already had a year of college under her belt. Kyle dressed in shades of black and mumbled on those rare occasions he opened his mouth, while everything about Alice was as bright and crisp as line-dried linens. Still, the physics of romance could not be denied. Kyle and Alice had pined for each other for over a year before she finally surrendered to the hormonal gravity between them, and now they were inseparable.

Alice wiggled a little in Kyle's grasp, more settling in than struggling. "Hey, Mr. Harper. I finished that biography of Virginia Wolfe you recommended. Pretty cool."

For a heartbeat, Finn stared at Alice as if she'd sprouted a second head. Then he muttered something about a deadline and, with a perfunctory wave in my direction, slipped around the teenagers and disappeared. I guess the fact that he wasn't technically family had suddenly hit home. Lord knows, a part of me wanted to run off with him. But the stricken look on Bree's face held me back.

"Jeez. What's everyone so glum about?" Alice asked.

During the moment of silence that followed, I watched the play of emotions on her elfin face. Her mischievous smile faded into puzzlement and then her cloudless eyes widened with dawning alarm.

"Mom?"

Peachy gave Bree a nudge. "It's gonna be all over town, Bree. No sense playing coy."

Bree caught my gaze, her eyes pleading with me to save her from this. It about broke my heart.

I couldn't spare her the talk with Alice, but I could provide her with a little privacy.

"Kyle," I said, "I know you're not on the schedule, but why don't we head back to the A-la-mode and spell Beth for a bit?"

Kyle looked down at the top of Alice's strawberry blond head. The lines of his lanky body drew taut. He wasn't a dumb kid. He had to know something was really wrong, and I loved him for wanting to protect Alice. But Finn had the right idea: this conversation was no place for anyone but family.

"Kyle?" I prodded. "Let's go."

Alice's lashes fluttered as she looked up at him. "It's okay," she whispered.

I took him by the arm, prying him away from his girl, and ushered him out of the booth. Without a word, we cut across the stretch of prairie grass behind the food stalls heading toward the asphalt pad where fair vendors could park. My beat-up GMC van held a prime spot on the near edge of that lot, and I smothered a sigh at giving it up.

Kyle hung back, dawdling, casting nervous glances back over his shoulder. Finally I heard the scuff of his Chuck Taylors in the sunbaked dirt as he stopped in his tracks.

I halted, too, and faced him.

"Miz Tally, do we really need to go to the A-la-mode?"

Like I said, the kid wasn't stupid.

"No," I conceded. "Actually, Beth needs the hours." As my business had picked up, I'd finally hired another employee, a wifty woman with a young son to support and no friends or family in town. With school starting in just a few weeks, she was scrambling to scrape together money for new clothes and supplies so her eight-year-old would blend with the wealthier kids.

Kyle glowered.

"We don't need to spell Beth, but we need to give Alice and Bree some space."

He shrugged. "I'm just gonna wait for her here. She might need me."

I sent up a silent prayer of thanks that Alice had someone to lean on right now. Rightly or wrongly, I knew Sonny's return to Dalliance—not to mention his denial of paternity—would put a strain on Alice's relationship with her mama. That's how mother-daughter relationships work, at least the ones in our family. No matter who's at fault, mom gets the blame. Until Alice had a chance to untangle her hurt and confusion, Bree would be public enemy number one.

"All right. But you wait outside. If you bust in there, I'll have your hide. And as long as you're waiting around, you can work the booth for a bit after they're done in there. I don't think Bree's gonna be in any kind of mood to scoop sundaes. So no tearing off with Alice in your hoopty old Bonneville." Kyle had recently inherited his big brother's '97 Pontiac Bonneville, which possessed an unsettlingly spacious backseat. "Bree's got enough to worry about," I muttered.

Kyle shoved his hands deep in his jeans pockets, ducked his head, and glared up at me through his lashes. His expression was standard-issue sullen teenage boy, but something about his eyes or the set of his jaw induced an eerie sense of déjà vu. Suddenly I was eighteen again, standing in the Tasty-Swirl parking lot in my white sundress, watching helplessly as my romance with Finn Harper disappeared in a spray of gravel and a squeal of tires.

I shook off the sense of doom that enveloped me, gave Kyle an impulsive hug, and took off in the direction of the Creative Arts Arena. I'd rounded the corner of the A-la-mode booth to make my way back to the midway when Finn stepped out of the shadows and took me by the arm.

"Tally."

"Lord a'mighty, Finn. You took a year off my life."

"Sorry. I just . . ." He trailed off, and his gaze drifted to a spot over my shoulder.

He looked so intense, I glanced behind me to see if anyone was coming, but we were alone.

"Is Alice okay?" he finally asked.

"I don't know. Bree's giving her the news right now. But don't let her little-girl looks fool you. Alice is a tough cookie. She'll muddle through."

He nodded, but his expression remained troubled.

"You working?" I asked.

"What?" He shook himself, and when his eyes met mine again the devilish glint had returned. "Actually, yes. I'm supposed to be doing a feature on the newcomers to the Lantana County Fair. The A-la-mode included."

He leaned in close and whispered in my ear, "Wanna preview that new haunted rodeo ride with me? It might be romantic."

I laughed. "What part of zombie cowboys and ghostly saloon girls is 'romantic'?"

His warm breath stirred the hair at my temple as he chuckled. "Come on. It'll be dark, and we can hold hands."

I knew I needed to get back to the Creative Arts building for a meeting with Garrett and Kristen about judging procedures and the timing of announcing various awards. And I knew that Bree and Alice might both need a little support—not to mention time off from the A-la-mode booth.

Finn laced his fingers with mine and tugged gently. I inhaled the clean bite of juniper and wintergreen that emanated from his skin. And I felt my resistance melt. There would be plenty of demands on my time over the next twenty-four hours, but I could afford to play hooky for fifteen minutes to slip away with my man.

Besides, I reasoned, the haunted rodeo was right on the way to the Creative Arts Arena.

The fairgrounds were laid out like a giant cross. When fairgoers entered the main gate to the south, they had to run a gantlet of carnival barkers challenging them to feats of strength and coordination in order to reach the midway rides—the carousel, the Ferris wheel, the Tilt-A-Whirl, the swings, the battle-ax, and, this year, the haunted rodeo. If you continued north through the rides, you'd reach the arena where the rodeo and pageants were held. To the west of the midway, the strip of food booths led to a small amphitheater where one-hit wonders and local honky-tonk bands put on free shows, while the Creative Arts buildings dominated the east side of the fairgrounds.

Finn and I held hands and dashed toward the midway, giggling like a couple of kids sneaking in after the prom.

Between the Tilt-A-Whirl and the carousel, perennial fair favorites, the new haunted rodeo attraction—Doc Lister's Wild, Wild West—hid behind a massive facade of weathered wood, swinging saloon doors, and a huge spectral cowboy whose animatronic gun arm rose and fell in time with the demented cackling of the ride's sound track.

The ride might be new to the Lantana County Fair, but it sure as heck wasn't new on this earth. In fact, the painted steel steps and pitted orange enameled cars looked as if they might date back to the dust bowl.

As we stepped onto the platform, it wobbled beneath our feet. I stopped and gave Finn a "you gotta be kidding me" look. He just grinned, cocked an eyebrow in a wicked dare, and tugged gently on my hand. He didn't come right out and call me a chicken, but I got the message.

A man stepped out from beneath the curtain of fake spiderweb and tattered bunting that draped down from the boot spurs of the giant zombie cowboy. I recognized Wiley Bishop. Wiley did odd jobs around town and always smelled a little like whiskey and bologna. He wore grease-stained dungarees and a faded Papa Smurf T-shirt, a blue bandanna tied around his head.

Silver bristles stuck straight out of the bit of scalp that showed, like the spines on a cactus, and deep crevices fanned across his face like the arroyos that scarred the high desert landscape. A dusting of red glitter across his cheekbone seemed wildly out of place.

As he approached, he sucked on his teeth, as though he were summoning the spit to speak.

"Come on up, folks. First passengers of the day." He coughed, a deep rattling cough, and I half expected to see a puff of dust belch from between his lips.

"Hey, Wiley," Finn said, "you got a little . . ." Finn touched his own cheek, prompting Wiley to rub his own face. Wiley's efforts removed a bit of the glitter, but left behind a bold slash of grease.

"Dang old whore," Wiley muttered.

"Wiley, there's a lady present," Finn warned.

"Naw, not a real whore. One a' them dummies inside. She kicks her legs over the tracks and the glitter come off her frilly skirts. Found some in my drawers last night." He sucked his teeth again, expressing his disgust for glittery undergarments. "Two tickets each."

Finn tore off four red tickets, the universal currency of the fair rides and games, and handed them to Wiley, who folded them accordion-style and tucked them in a hot-pink fanny pack that rested on his hip. Finn held my hand as I stepped down from the platform to the dusty bench seat before joining me. His hand brushed my hip as he pulled the seat belt across my body and snapped it together between us.

He leaned close and whispered in my ear, "You can hold my hand if you get scared."

I gave him the stink eye. "Oh, sure, I'm quaking in my boots already."

The six-car train started forward with a bone-jarring lurch. Somewhere above us, speakers emitted tinny cackles and "yee-haws," and plinking piano music. As we chugged along through scenes of Main Street shoot-outs and positively offensive Indian tableaus—complete with "hey-a-hey-a" chanting and tomahawk chops— the whole experience registered more as "confusing" and "loud" than "scary." The only redeeming features of the ride were the puffs of cool, spooky mist and the dark.

Finn took full advantage of the dark.

We finally rounded a corner into an old-fashioned saloon. The fakey piano music picked up again, but this stretch of the ride was quieter than the others. A ghoulish bartender polished the same glass over and over while a table of zombie cowboys rocked back and forth over a game of cards and a bottle of whiskey. The piano and its ghostly player nestled against the far wall, right next to a set of old-fashioned saloon doors. Oddly, a small balcony teetered above the doors, and a saloon girl perched there, kicking her leg just out of sync with the music. Even in the dim light, I could see the sparkle of the red glitter that plagued poor Wiley in the girl's tulle skirts. In one last hurrah, a crazed cowboy with red glowing eyes burst through the saloon's swinging doors, guns blazing with puffs of white smoke. Canned shrieks rang out, and the cardplayers collapsed over their hands.

I smothered a laugh as Finn kissed the ticklish spot

right behind my ear. The train gave a last jerking push toward the exit. For a moment, we were in total darkness.

Finn whispered something into the tender skin at my temple.

"What?"

I felt his lips curl in a smile. He dipped his head to get closer to my ear and whispered again, "I love you."

I froze. Ahead of us, I could see the light leaking around the exit door, and we were moving closer and closer. I wanted so bad to stop the whole world, make everything hold still so I could savor those words. For nearly twenty years, I'd only heard those words from Finn in the deepest, most secret corners of my mind. And there they were, just out there. I wanted to touch those words, hold them in my hand, feel the weight and reality of them.

But the exit door, haloed in light, grew closer.

I should have said the words back, made the circle complete right there in that sacred moment, but I had no air for words. Instead, I twisted around, groped for his hair, and pulled his head down into a heated kiss . . . hoping that every ounce of my joy and terror and love was communicated from flesh to flesh.

The train nudged through the ride's exit, and we pulled apart as the harsh summer sunlight blinded our dark-adjusted eyes.

# *chapter 4*

After Finn's bombshell, he had to dash off to do reporterly things. I had mustered the nerve to head back into the fray at the Creative Arts Exhibit, but my phone vibrated to indicate I had a new voice mail message—apparently there wasn't any cell reception inside the haunted rodeo. I checked the call record as I dialed in. Garrett Simms.

He assured me that the great ice cream controversy had been settled: Tucker's Pepper Praline ice cream used cayenne instead of ancho chili, and his praline was more brown sugary than the dulce de leche in my Texas Twister.

It seemed Tucker Gentry, who had swept the yellow tomato canning categories and won best in show for his tomato-pepper-tequila jam the year before, could hold his head high in this year's cooking contests.

Garrett sighed. "I knew I couldn't make everyone happy with that decision, but apparently I didn't make anyone happy. Tucker's still moping around here like a lovelorn teenage girl, and Eloise is on the warpath. She's mighty peeved at you for, and I quote, 'not defending your own blasted ice cream.' I'm getting out of here for the day, and I suggest you lie low, too."

His advice suited me fine, as I wanted some quiet time to savor Finn's sweet confession.

I left Kyle sulking over setting up the A-la-mode booth and handling the first night's customers—despite a promise I would send Beth in to help him—and took Peachy and Bree back to the store on the Dalliance Courthouse Square.

While Bree and Peachy ran out for our dinner, I busied myself making a giant batch of bittersweet fudge for the next day. I let the narcotic scent of warm chocolate seep into my pores while I replayed those moments in the haunted rodeo over and over.

Peachy's brittle voice broke through my blissful haze. "Barbecue," she barked, announcing the evening's menu.

"Oh, good. I'm starved."

I was, too. Between the hubbub over Tucker's ice cream, Sonny's return to Dalliance, and my little interlude with Finn, I'd missed lunch.

We clustered around one of the café tables in the front of the store—just in case a customer drifted in while we were eating—and tucked into dinner from Erma's Fry by Night Diner: barbecued brisket sandwiches, laced with homemade bread and butter pickles and sweet onions, and fresh coleslaw.

While Peachy and I mulled over her competition in the quilt show and debated whether the Lantana Round-Up Rodeo Queen Pageant demeaned women or not, Bree listlessly poked at her coleslaw and looked as if her best dog died. I couldn't even coax a smile from her with one of her favorite black Irish milk shakes (dark chocolate ice cream laced with Irish cream).

As predicted, Alice hadn't taken the news of Sonny's return and the paternity suit particularly well. She'd skedaddled off in a huff, refusing even the comfort Kyle offered. With nothing but a backpack and bicycle, she couldn't get into too much trouble. I knew our girl: she'd go blow off some steam, talk herself from raging to rational, and turn up at home as if nothing had happened.

In her head, Bree knew that, too. But her heart wasn't so sure.

"She's gonna hate me," she mourned, while I went ahead and added an extra glug of Irish cream to the milk shake container.

"For what?" Peachy snapped. "You didn't do anything but love her every day of her life. If she's gonna hate anyone, it's that snake Sonny." She smacked her hand on the wrought-iron café table. "I wish to God he wasn't her daddy."

"Bite your tongue, Gram. Sonny's Alice's father, and I'm going to prove it." She reached into the mammoth purse at her feet and hauled out a small plastic sandwich bag.

From the other side of our wide marble counter, I had to squint to make out the bag's contents: a small plastic cup, like the kind that comes with bottles of cough syrup, and a lime green plastic spoon.

Peachy, too, was squinting at Bree's hands. "Lord a'mighty, child, what do you have?"

"I snagged that little sample of caramel Sonny tasted. I'm gonna send it off for DNA."

Peachy frowned. "Why don't you leave all that stuff to the courts? You shoulda got a judge in the middle of this fifteen years ago. That's what courts are for, Sabrina Marie."

"I know, Gram. But my friend Andi down at the Bar None, her daughter got knocked up and didn't know who the daddy was. It took four months to find out. Those state labs are all backed up with murders and stuff. Andi said there was a private lab where they could have sent the samples and gotten results in less than a week. But Andi's daughter didn't have the money."

She looked at me hard. Even from across the room, I could feel the raw force of her will. "I'm not about to wait four months."

I sighed. "Bree, you know I'll get you the money. Even if I have to sell a kidney. But I bet the courts don't accept that kind of evidence. I mean, I don't think Kristen Ver Steeg's going to just take your word for it that that little green spoon has Sonny's spit on it. Do you?"

She shrugged. "Don't know, don't care. That fancy-pants Kristen Ver Steeg can take her legal mumbo jumbo and shove it where the sun don't shine. This isn't about a lawsuit or child support. This is about giving my little girl her daddy back."

The next morning, Bree and I left Alice sleeping off her emotional bender and Peachy shoring up our domestic defenses with zucchini muffins and butterscotch bars.

Bree disappeared the minute we got to the fairgrounds, so my newest hire, Beth Oldman, and I got the fudge and caramel sauces heating in their water baths and fired up the waffle cone presses.

"Will you be okay here alone for a few minutes?"

Beth surveyed the tiny space within the booth. Hair the rich burnished brown of espresso beans curled around her square jaw, and she tucked it back behind her ear. "Sure thing. Can't hardly fit two people back here, anyway."

"Thanks, Beth. I don't know where Bree got off to, and I really need to head over to the Creative Arts Exhibit and talk to Garrett about the judging schedule. He wants the committee to meet about the canned goods and the quilts next Wednesday evening, and that conflicts with the big karaoke contest. Bree will have my hide if I'm not there for her big moment."

I don't know why I was nattering on. Beth had already turned her back on me and was obsessively stacking and restacking the metal milk shake canisters.

She was an odd duck, for sure. I didn't know where Beth and her son, Sam, had come from, at least not recently. Occasionally Sam talked about ships and the ocean, and I thought I detected a trace of Boston in

Beth's voice, but I got the sense they'd been moving a lot. Beth herself never offered any personal information, and I sure didn't want to intrude. All that really mattered was that, as distracted and neurotic as she seemed, Beth was a crackerjack employee.

As I cut across the midway on my way to the other side of the fairgrounds, I ran into Detective Cal McCormack.

Literally. Ran smack into him. Which was a little like barreling headfirst into a mountain.

Cal and I had a long history together. Throughout grade school and high school, he'd been my honorary big brother. We'd drifted apart as adults, but a few months before, we'd gotten pretty close again. I hurt Cal a lot when I started dating Finn, but he wasn't the type of man to hold a grudge. He made no bones about the fact that he disapproved of Finn Harper and thought I was a fool to let him back into my life, but he wasn't mean about it. In fact, he was pretty tight-lipped around me. Civil, though.

"What brings you out to the fair today?" I said.

"Meeting," he responded. Cal wasn't much of a talker. But the way he looked over my shoulder when he said it and the flush creeping up his neck told me there was more to the story.

"Cal McCormack. Spill it. What kind of meeting could possibly bring you out here at this hour? And put that blush on your face, to boot?"

He swept the cowboy hat from his head and ran his long, square fingers through his neat salt-and-pepper hair. Cal always dressed as if he were heading to an old-fashioned barn dance: well-laundered jeans, a crisp cotton shirt tucked in with military precision, nicely polished boots. A cowboy, all cleaned up. That morning, he wore his shirt buttoned to his clean-shaven chin and a bolo tie around his neck. The only thing marring the Sunday-best image was his shoulder holster and gun.

"Don't laugh, but I got roped into being a judge for the Lantana Round-Up Rodeo Queen Pageant." He gave me a hard look. "I told you not to laugh."

"Cal McCormack, you can't tell me you're judging a beauty pageant and expect me to keep a straight face. I mean, I can see you judging the marksmanship competitions, or the roping, or even picking the best blackberry jam, but a beauty pageant?"

He tipped his head, and I heard his vertebrae crack. "It's not a beauty pageant. They're judged on character and horsemanship and . . ." He cleared his throat.

"And beauty. You can say it. Just because those girls wear big ol' belt buckles over their evening gowns doesn't make it any less of a beauty pageant. They still have the teased-up hair. Just with a hat perched on top of it."

He narrowed his eyes and opened his mouth as though he were about to argue with me.

"Come on, Cal. Do we need to break out the dictionary?"

Cal was forever complaining that I needed a dictionary because my definition of little things like "truth" and "meddling" didn't quite square up with his.

He cracked a smile then. A little one, but a smile

nonetheless. "Well, whatever you call it, the coordinator, this attorney named Kristen Ver Steeg—"

"Yeah, I know Kristen," I muttered.

"She was mighty persuasive, and, uh, before I knew what I was doing I said yes."

I could imagine exactly how that conversation went: Kristen looking up at Cal through her long lashes, a soft curl of platinum hair curling around her delicate jaw, as she begged his favor. Cal getting all "ma'amy" and uptight and maybe even blushing a bit.

"Mmm-hmm," I mused. "Was she 'persuasive' like Madeline Albright? Or persuasive like Pamela Anderson?"

"Don't be smart." He cleared his throat. "I'm not even all that partial to blondes. Still, here I am."

"I thought the pageant started on Friday."

"It does," Cal said. "But Kristen called all the judges yesterday and said we needed to meet right away. Some kind of emergency."

"Sounds dramatic," I said with a smirk.

He rolled his broad shoulders. "I don't know what's going on. All I know is I ought to be working. You know, catching criminals."

"Well, I should let you get to your meeting," I said. "It looks like Kristen is on her way."

Cal turned around so he, too, could see Kristen Ver Steeg, once again in a sleek, fashionable, impractically cream-colored suit, hustling up the midway from the main entrance of the fairgrounds.

Cal raised a hand in greeting, but Kristen didn't see us.

She was making a beeline for, of all things, the haunted rodeo ride.

Cal and I shared a puzzled glance, then watched as she took the rickety steps of the ride in her ridiculous sling-back heels, handed something to a slack-jawed Wiley, and then stepped into the first car on the ride's train without any apparent regard for her beautiful suit.

I was still processing Kristen's bizarre behavior when, amazingly, I saw Bree dashing up the same set of stairs. Her valentine hair and bodacious curves were unmistakable as she piled into the car behind Kristen's. Wiley shook his head as he walked back to the control box and worked his magic. Within a heartbeat, the sound track for the ride powered up and, amid the cackling and hooting, the cars carrying Bree and Kristen disappeared into the ride.

"Snow White and Rose Red," Cal murmured.

I turned my attention back to him. "What?"

He shook his head. "Nothing. Just a fairy tale. Snow White and Rose Red. They kill a bear and marry a dwarf. Or something. I don't remember. The two of them together made me think of it, is all."

"So that was weird, right?"

He shrugged. "I don't really expect normal anymore."

I laughed. "That's probably wise. Well, I guess this means your meeting's going to be a little late."

He grimaced, but didn't answer.

And just that quickly, we ran out of conversation. I felt a twinge of sorrow that the friendship we had built at the beginning of the summer could have withered away so quickly. I met Cal's eyes and saw my regret mirrored there. Somehow knowing that he, too, felt the strain between us, and knowing that he knew that I knew . . . it intensified the awkwardness tenfold.

"Well, uh," I stammered, trying to come up with a graceful way to say good-bye.

Something stopped me, mouth open, midword. My conscious brain didn't register the change right away, but then I realized that the hokey sound track from the haunted rodeo had stopped. In the sudden and unexpected silence, a woman screamed. Not the tinny shriek from the ride's recorded narrative, but a real, flesh-and-blood holler. And then a sound—a brisk *crack*—sent a jolt of electric fear through my entire body, as if someone had sent pure current into the most primal curl of my brain.

A gunshot.

I'd barely formed the thought before Cal pushed me aside and sprinted toward the haunted rodeo. I was right behind him. Bree needed me.

Cal leaped onto the ride's platform in a single bound, boots ringing the sheet metal like a bell as his body weight crashed down. He dodged around Wiley, who stood frozen, staring slack-jawed at the fake wood door of the ride's exit. Cal paused at the door, setting his back against the wall beside it.

Another shot rang out, the sound unmistakable this close.

He drew his weapon. "Call 911," he barked at Wiley.

Then, cautiously, he pried open the door and peered inside, eyes squinted against the darkness within.

I took the stairs two at a time. When I reached the top, Cal glanced in my direction. "You. Stay the hell back."

The stripped-down tension in his voice gave me pause, but as soon as he disappeared into the haunted rodeo, I crept to the door behind him.

At first, with my eyes not yet adjusted, the interior of the attraction appeared pitch-black. But, by feel, I could tell there was a narrow ledge on either side of the depression for the tracks, presumably for maintenance and emergencies like this one. I felt my way along that ledge, sliding one foot out carefully before inching the rest of my body along.

After several painstaking minutes, my eyes adjusted. There was enough light from the saloon tableau, the last one on the ride, to make out the contours of the ledge and to see Cal just a few feet ahead of me and on the other side of the tunnel. He was paused at the opening to the saloon, craning his head as he scanned the interior.

As I closed the distance between us, Cal suddenly shifted, pressing his back against the side of the tunnel, struggling in vain to make his broad shoulders less of a target.

"Put the gun down," Cal said, his tone hard as granite.

I could hear weeping from deeper in the room. Weeping and gasping.

"I said, put the gun down."

"No, no, no."

I sagged against the wall in relief. Bree's voice. At least she was alive.

But she continued to murmur no like an incantation. Like a child huddled beneath the covers willing away the bogeyman with the sheer force of her fear.

"Bree, you need to do what I say now."

"No, not till he's gone."

"Till who's gone?"

"Him," she hissed.

"Him, who?" I'd never thought of Cal as a patient man, mostly because I managed to rile him so easily. But in the face of Bree's crazy talk, he remained firm but calm.

"Him," she said again. "By the door. With the gun."

Cal dropped into a crouch and edged close enough to the tunnel entrance to peer around the corner.

I could hear him sigh.

"Bree, that man's not real. He's just part of the ride."

"No," Bree insisted. "He shot at us. For real. He shot at me and . . ." Bree's voice trailed off, and then she screamed again.

All rational thought vanished. Bree's terror triggered pure instinct and I scooted past Cal, leaped the tracks, and plunged headfirst into the saloon.

I saw Bree right away, crouched next to the poker-playing zombie cowboys, her flame-colored topknot impossible to miss. As I got closer, I saw she held a long-barreled gun clutched in her hands.

"Bree?" I said. "Honey?"

"Dammit, Tally," Cal snapped, only a pace behind me. "Get down."

I ignored him and knelt by Bree's side.

"Tally!" Cal barked. "She's got a gun."

"She's scared spitless, Cal. She's not going to shoot me."

To punctuate my claim, Bree threw the gun away, sending it skittering across the floor. I heard Cal mutter to himself—"Can't you do just one little goddamn thing I tell you to? Just one?"—but I kept my eyes fixed firmly on Bree.

Between her bloodless complexion, the dark wounds of her smeared mascara, and the fiery halo cast by the ride's spotlights sparking her crimson hair, Bree looked as if she'd crawled right out of a horror movie. She reached for me with grasping hands, and, without hesitation, I pulled her close. She leaned her body into mine, trembling like a newborn colt. I crooned nonsense words in her ear, held her tight against me, and rocked her.

From near the tracks, I heard Cal cuss. I looked over to where he stood. Kristen Ver Steeg lay sprawled, half in and half out of the train's front car, a dark stain spreading across her impractical cream suit.

I met Cal's eyes. He shook his head. Then his gaze slid to the right, to Bree, who continued to cry quietly.

Kristen was dead. And the only living soul who'd seen her die was Bree.

# chapter 5

Police and emergency personnel descended on the haunted rodeo within minutes. By the time the uniformed authorities rushed in and began processing the scene, Bree stood on her own two feet and had a little of her pepper back.

One of the cops, a kid with sunburned scalp shining beneath his buzz cut and acne putting a permanent blush on his baby-round cheeks, approached Bree with a long cotton swab in one hand and a little fear in his eyes.

"Whatcha planning to do with that, sugar?" Bree asked, a smile simmering on her lips. "You haven't even bought me dinner."

The young officer looked helplessly at Cal.

"Bree. Behave."

She rolled her eyes. "Jeez. Cut me some slack. Someone just tried to kill me, for cryin' out loud. I'm not serious."

Cal crossed his arms across his chest. "Most folks would be serious as a heart attack if they were standing in your shoes."

"Well, I'm not most people." Bree extended one leg and admired her three-inch-high strappy gold sandals. "Most people wouldn't look quite so fine standing in these shoes."

"Bree," I hissed. "Hush."

I knew my cousin better than I knew myself. She was still scared as all heck, but she'd always fallen back on humor when she felt cornered.

I knew it was a defense mechanism. Cal might not. And Cal was the one with the handcuffs.

Bree sighed and held out her hands so the young man could swab them.

While Bree submitted to the ministrations of the crime techs and photographers snapped pictures of poor Kristen's body, Cal grabbed me by the elbow and pulled me aside.

"You," he barked, indicating a female officer who was hanging back from the crowd. "I want you to set up a perimeter around that . . . uh, that zombie over there."

"Sir?"

"You heard me. The one with the hat and the gun. Make sure no one messes in that part of the room until the crime scene guys can process it."

She scurried away to do his bidding, and Cal turned that frown on me. "Tally, you make me crazy."

I sighed. "I know, Cal. I'm sorry."

"No, you're not."

I sighed again. "I'm not sorry for what I did, but I am sorry I make you crazy. I just couldn't stand back while Bree was in trouble."

He shook his head. "She's still in trouble. A passel of it."

I pulled out of his grasp and stepped back. "You don't think she had anything to do with this."

His right eyebrow cocked up. "Tally, she's smack in the middle of it. We both saw her chase after Kristen and pile into the ride right behind her, right?"

"She wasn't chasing Kristen. You heard her. Kristen asked to meet her here this morning. They happened to be going to the same place—at Kristen's suggestion—and Kristen got there first."

"Mmm-hmm. Right. And we both heard her say she and Kristen were alone in here when the shots were fired."

I held up a hand. "No way. She did not say they were alone. She said there was a man in here with them."

"Oh, right," Cal said, his voice thick with sarcasm. "The man with the gun. Except she only saw one figure in that doorway, and he's still standing there: a plastic zombie cowboy and his plastic gun. That gun *she* was holding, on the other hand, that's the real deal. Serial number's been filed off, so who knows who owns the thing? But it was in Bree's hands, Tally. It'll take a while for ballistics to check the bullet that killed Kristen against that weapon, but if it's a match . . . well, she's in trouble."

I gave him a narrow look, trying to see behind his

bluster to what was really going on in his mind. "You're pretty quick to dismiss the plastic cowboy, but you told that lady cop to keep an eye on it."

He looked past me, and when I followed his line of sight I realized he was looking at Bree.

"Just doing my job, Tally. I have to preserve evidence if there is any, and if there isn't . . . I have to tell a judge and jury, with a straight face, that I looked."

I'd seen Cal's softer side at the beginning of the summer. I knew it was buried down deep beneath that tough-guy shell. And I thought I detected a glimmer of it as he stared at my cousin. My cousin who appeared to be blowing into a Breathalyzer at that very moment.

Interesting.

"When can I take her home?" I asked.

"What?" Cal jerked his attention back to me. "Oh. We need to take her down to the station to get her official statement. You, too, actually."

Lord a'mighty. In the past year, I'd seen more of the inside of the Dalliance Police Station than any law-abiding citizen should.

*Dang*, I thought. *Here we go again.*

# *chapter 6*

After I gave my statement to the cops, I waited at the station for Bree. They'd brought her in in the back of a Dalliance PD cruiser—providing a photo op sure to make the front page of the next day's *News-Letter*—so I drove her back to the fairgrounds in my van.

While I navigated around the courthouse square to head north to the fairgrounds, Bree was quiet. A scratchy cassette tape of Dolly Parton was working its way through my stereo, and Dolly wailed about the man-greedy Jolene, until Bree stabbed the button to shut off the music.

"So," I said as I turned onto North Hazlett, "are you gonna tell me what happened in there?"

Bree was looking out her side window, so I couldn't see her face, but she sniffed softly. "I'm in big trouble."

"So what's new?" I quipped, trying to draw her out.

"No, this is real bad, Tally. She asked me to meet her at the ride, I swear. But the cops don't believe me."

"If she called, there must be phone records."

"They checked her phones—home, cell, office—and there's no call to me."

"What about your cell records? Just show them the incoming call."

"She called me on my home line."

Bree and Alice lived with me in my crumbling 1925 Arts and Crafts bungalow. Even though we all had cell phones, we'd kept the two landlines into the house. Habit, partly, and insurance against losing the phones or letting their batteries die (which happened with alarming regularity). One of the phones was in the kitchen—the house phone, we called it—and the other was in Bree's room, a room that used to belong to the previous owner's teenage daughter.

"How'd she even get that number?" We kept those old-fashioned phones, but we hardly ever used them. We were all out and about so much, we usually relied on the cells.

"I don't know. The cops said they'll pull the records for the landline, but I could tell they're just humoring me. They think I'm lying. After all, I was holding the gun."

"But I saw them swab your hands for gunshot residue. That'll prove you didn't shoot her."

Bree crumpled in the seat, her shoulders hunched over in pure misery. "The residue test was positive."

I slammed on the brakes, causing the driver in the

car behind me to lay on the horn and swerve around me. The driver threw me the finger as he sped away. I pulled the van to the side of the road, parking it in front of Dalliance's new natural birthing center.

"Did the stupid crime tech guys mess up?" I demanded.

"No. I did shoot the gun."

"You what?"

"I shot the gun. I just didn't shoot it at Kristen." Bree slapped her hand against the dashboard. "It all happened so fast."

"Okay, walk me through it," I soothed.

"The little train car was making its way through the ride. Kristen was trying to talk to me from her seat in front of me, but I don't think she figured it would be so loud in there. I couldn't hear a word she said. But she looked mighty pissed, and she kept shaking her head.

"When we pulled into that last room, there was a crack, the train car suddenly jolted to a stop, and the music died. The detective I talked to told me it looked like a bullet hit a power box, shutting down parts of the ride. Anyway, I freaked. I hit the dirt. I mean literally, down on the floor of that grimy car. The only thing I heard was the crash of the saloon doors swinging open and that zombie cowboy sliding in on his track. Then there was a pop, like a shot, and someone screamed. I think it was me. I think."

Bree hugged her arms around her body, and I reached out to lay a comforting hand on her shoulder.

"I heard a clatter, and from where I was in the bottom of the car, I saw that gun skitter across the floor. I don't know what I was thinking, but I scrambled out on all fours, grabbed the gun, and when I peeked over the poker table, I saw a man. Or I thought I saw a man. Maybe it was just the dummy zombie. But I was scared, so I shot at him."

She looked at me. "I fired the gun, Tally. Away from Kristen, but the cops don't believe that. The gun's a revolver, so there aren't any shell casings to prove where anyone was standing when they fired the gun. Every shred of physical evidence points to me. And the whole dang fair saw her serve me with papers just yesterday.

"Tally, I'm scared."

I leaned across the seat and hugged her tight. We were too close for lies. "I'm scared, too, Bree. But I'm right by your side, you hear?"

That night we left Kyle and Beth working the booth at the fairgrounds and the whole family—Bree, Alice, Peachy, and I—retreated to the A-la-mode and holed up, waiting for a siege.

Sure enough, just before eight, Sonny Anders and his new lady friend paid us a visit.

Bree's close call had triggered an early truce in the mother-daughter conflict, and Bree and Alice were in the back of the store, their arms tangled in a needy hug as they watched ice cream form in my special vertical batch freezers. Peachy had camped out on a chair in the back, unwilling to take her eyes off either one of them.

That left me to serve as welcoming party.

Ha.

They took their time strolling into the store, Sonny making a big production of looking around, so I took my time sizing them up.

I was particularly interested in Sonny's female companion. I have to admit, the woman had it going on: copper hair piled atop her head, porcelain skin, legs up to her armpits, and a body like a men's mag centerfold, all perky peaks and seductive valleys. She wore a twilight gray suit that clung to every curve, a wide belt of creamy leather cinched at her waist, and impossibly tall heels. I knew that look drove men crazy, all prim and proper but with the suggestion that pulling just one hair pin from her tidy French twist would unleash a total vixen.

When I met her gaze, I saw a mix of curiosity and calculation.

Sonny's new girl wasn't just arm candy. There was a brain behind all that beauty. I could see it in her eyes.

"Hey there, Tally," Sonny said, a big ol' grin spreading across his face like an oil slick. "I see you've spruced up the Dippery."

For years, an ice cream parlor had occupied our spot on the Dalliance Courthouse Square. During my lifetime, it had been Dave's Dippery. It just happened that David Thompson decided to move to San Antonio to be closer to his grandkids at about the same time I split with my ex, Wayne Jones. I took over Dave's lease, bought most of his equipment, supplemented it with my specialty French pot ice cream makers, and the A-la-mode was born.

"What do you want, Sonny?"

He shivered. "Brrrr. Must be all that ice cream. It's mighty chilly in here."

I swallowed a cussword. For Alice's sake, I needed to be civil to this slimeball. "Sorry. I'm just guessing you aren't here for a banana split."

His eyes narrowed for a second, but then his grin cranked up to full power. "You guess right. I was hoping to see my g—"

The redhead knocked her hip into Sonny, cutting him off.

He cleared his throat. "Is Alice here?"

I didn't answer him directly, because I wasn't sure how Bree wanted me to play this. "Just a minute."

I hustled to the back of the store, where Alice and Bree were packing pints with a batch of our Rusted Roof ice cream: cinnamon ice cream dotted with slivers of smoked almonds and flakes of dark chocolate.

I dragged Bree aside as discreetly as I could and whispered in her ear, "Sonny's here. With the woman. Wants to see Alice."

Bree's arm tensed beneath my fingers. "Well, let's get this over with."

She pulled away from me and returned to Alice's side. "Honey," she said softly, "your daddy's here. He wants to see you. But if you want us to send him away, we will."

Alice's body grew utterly still, but she looked her mama in the eye. "I told you I want to see him."

"I know. I just thought you might change your mind." I could hear the hope in Bree's voice, the quiet prayer that her daughter would stay away from Sonny Anders.

Alice shook her head and headed for the front of the store with Bree, Peachy, and me right behind her.

Sonny froze when he saw Alice. Even from across the room, I could see his Adam's apple slide up and down his throat as he studied her. Although her hair and eyes were lighter, and her frame was a bit more petite, Alice had her mama's looks. For Sonny, seeing her must have been like seeing a pale reflection of the Bree he had married all those years ago

Alice stared at her daddy the way she stared at a particularly intractable math problem. Her sweet, child-like features remained utterly expressionless, but her clear aqua eyes blazed with determination.

I could only guess what she was looking for in his face. An echo of something familiar. A primal recognition of kinship. A glimmer of sorrow or regret. Something to make sense both of his absence and his return.

"Hey, baby." Sonny managed to smile as if this were no big deal, just another "howdy" in his busy social calendar, but his voice betrayed his nerves. Apparently he wasn't totally heartless after all.

"Hello," Alice answered, carefully formal.

"Uh . . ." Sonny rocked back on his heels and dug his hands in his pants pockets. He puckered up as if he was gonna whistle a tune, but then tipped his head toward the woman at his side. "This here's Char."

Alice's mouth got tight as if she was trying to hold something in. Then a little burble of laughter escaped. "Cher? Sonny and Cher?"

The redhead's mouth, held in a carefully neutral smile, tightened at the corners.

"Ha!" Sonny barked, as if he'd never hear the joke before. "No, no, not Cher. Char."

"Charlize," the redhead clarified, her tone and accent as neutral as Switzerland. "Like the actress."

"How you been, baby?"

Alice frowned. "How've I been? You mean recently? Or all my life?"

Oh boy.

Bree reached out, grabbed my hand, and squeezed. I did the same to Peachy. We all braced ourselves for the coming storm.

Sonny's smile faltered, then hardened. "Show your daddy a little respect."

"Of course," Alice snapped. "You seen him around?" She swiveled her head around as if she were looking for something, then straightened up in mock surprise. "Oh, you mean *you*!" She snorted. "I thought my daddy was the subject of litigation."

"I'm just making sure, baby. That's the smart thing to do. I hear you're a real smart girl, so I'm sure you understand. Let a judge figure everything out."

Alice laughed. "You're right. That is smart. And until a judge tells me you're my father, you're nothing to me."

A flush licked up Sonny's neck. "Yeah, well, I may not be your daddy, but right now I'm the closest you got."

"Not true," Alice said. "Mr. Harper's been more of a dad to me than you could ever be."

Bree nearly crushed my fingers in her grip. We'd both seen plenty of Alice's righteous indignation and raw fury, but it was always directed at her mom and we knew it was just teenagery hormones. But this was the real deal, our girl's deepest pain on display. It was as if she'd opened a vein in the middle of the A-la-mode, and it was brutal to watch.

"At most you gave me your DNA," she continued. "And that's fine by me. I don't want anything else from you. So you can drop your stupid lawsuit, because I wouldn't take one red cent from you. Not now, not ever."

Alice's chin ticked up a notch. "It was nice meeting you, Miz Charlize. Welcome to Dalliance." She whirled around, pushed her way between me and Bree, and retreated to the back of the store.

Bree and Peachy exchanged a look, and Gram limped after Alice. It was a good call on Bree's part. As worked up as Alice was, Peachy's stolid presence would be a better comfort than Bree or me.

"Nice work, Sonny," Bree said. "You handled that like a pro."

"Listen," he said, "I'm doing the best I can." He glanced nervously at Charlize. "Darlin', could you give us a minute?"

A muscle twitched at the corner of her right eye, but Charlize batted her lashes and smiled. "Sure thing, sugar. I'll just go powder my nose."

She looked at me with an eyebrow raised in question, and I pointed toward the hallway leading to the ladies' room. She sashayed away. Bree hadn't lied: Beneath the fine wool suiting, there was a hypnotic sway to the woman's hips. Just a hint of something a bit improper.

As Char disappeared from view, Sonny sidled up to the counter.

It was as if a mask had slipped from his face. Suddenly he appeared earnest, worried. "Was Alice serious? Y'all don't want any money?"

A stillness settled over Bree's features. "Why?"

"Look, I don't want to make waves for you and Alice. Believe it or not, I don't want to see either of you get hurt. If you're not looking for a handout, I don't see any reason to drag us all through the courts."

"Are you serious?" Bree asked.

I could hear the edge of outrage in her voice, clear as a summer day, but apparently Sonny couldn't.

"Absolutely." He reached inside his suit jacket and pulled out a folded piece of paper. "I'm real glad you're here. If you'll just sign this paper, I'll get out of your hair."

"And what exactly would I be signing?"

Dang, if Sonny couldn't hear the river of ice in Bree's tone, he was a bigger idiot than I thought.

He licked his lips in a way that made me think he was starting to understand his error. But he soldiered on.

"It's just a promise that you won't sue me. You don't sue me, I won't sue you. Sounds fair, right?"

"Mmm." To me, that noncommittal hum sounded like the vibration of a teakettle right before it blows.

"I'm serious, Bree. I have to protect my interests,

but if you're not going after my money, then me claiming Alice doesn't do no harm."

I took a step back out of self-preservation. Mount Bree was about to blow.

She drew herself up, her chest swelling with indignation, her nostrils flaring with fury. Despite her strappy gold sandals and skimpy lavender polka-dot sundress, she was a Valkyrie, an Amazon, a warrior of pure feminine power, her flaming hair and arctic eyes burning with elemental rage.

"Wouldn't do no harm? You no-good, dried-up piece of cow crap, that girl is the only good thing you've ever done in your whole entire life. You should fall down and kiss the ground in gratitude that you get to 'claim' Alice as yours. God knows, you don't deserve her."

"I—"

She leaned forward on her toes, crowding Sonny and forcing him back a step. "No, sir, you just keep your lips zipped. It's my turn. I was hurt—hurt as hell—that you would question whether Alice was your child. But heck, I wasn't a saint. Maybe, just maybe, you were justified in questioning me. But now, come to find out, this isn't about anything other than money? Sonny Anders, I never figured you'd be so low. How dare you?"

Sonny's eyes darted to the side, as if he was worried about someone else—Alice? Charlize?—coming in and hearing his scolding. He sucked his teeth.

"Listen, Bree, you've got a right to be mad. But I worked hard for what I've got. Char and I, we've both worked hard. We're fixin' to get married, so any claim on my money is a claim on Char's, too. She stuck by me through some tough times."

"Oh, and loyalty means so much to you, huh?"

Sonny closed his eyes, silently accepting the gibe. "Look," he said, his voice lower, more reasonable, "I owe her. I have an obligation to protect her interests. You gotta understand that."

Bree snorted. "I don't gotta understand anything. I just have to hold your feet to the fire and make you be a man. Your first, last, and only obligation is to your child. Alice has gone without so many times—she couldn't go to science camp, she couldn't go on the class trip to Washington, D.C., she had to buy her prom dress at a secondhand store—and she's never complained. Not even once. And now she's managed to cobble together the scholarships to go to a fancy private college, but even so, she doesn't have the fast computer she needs or the chance to study abroad.

"You've never given her a damn thing. Alice may want to keep it that way, but it's not her call. It's mine. And I'll let you drag my name through the mud until the cows come home if it means prying some cash from your wallet so that child can have the education she deserves. The freakin' *life* she deserves. Because that girl is better and more important than you and I put together could ever hope to be."

Bree drew back her head, and for a second I thought she was going to spit in Sonny's face. But, instead, she turned on her heel and stalked away as fast as her stilettos could carry her.

"Sonny, I think maybe we should go."

Sometime during Bree's tirade, Char had slipped back into the room. A smile still graced her perfectly symmetrical face, but there was an unmistakable edge in her voice. She had to be completely mortified at her man acting like such a petty scuzz-bucket.

Sonny cleared his throat. "Sure thing, sugar."

Char sashayed forward, that wicked wiggle in her walk, and looped her arm through the crook of Sonny's elbow. "See ya, Tally," he said as they headed for the door.

He paused on the sidewalk, his hand still on the knob, the door still ajar. I watched him pat Char's arm, then gently pry her fingers from his sleeve.

He hustled back to the counter, Char watching him through the glass with narrowed eyes.

"Tally," he whispered. "Try to talk some sense into Bree. Get her to sign that release."

"Are you kidding me?"

"Look, I know you probably hate me. That's fine. But trust me. It'd be better if she signed that release."

I didn't respond, just crossed my arms over my chest.

He rolled his lips between his teeth and ran a hand through his hair, clearly frustrated. "You two are peas in a pod, aren't you? Stubborn as a rusty pump."

He hitched his hands in his pockets and left again. As he walked away, I turned my attention to Char. Her eyes were fixed on Sonny, her guard down. Her lower lip sagged in a bit of a pout, and the angle of her brows looked anxious to me.

I wondered again at their relationship. Sonny was a good-looking guy, in his own unctuous way, but Char seemed way out of his league. Yet she seemed strangely dependent on him, clinging to him, touching him, clutching him with her greedy gaze.

I suppose I shouldn't have been surprised. After all, Sonny had managed to seduce Bree—who was way smarter than she let on. Despite her big brain and rockin' bod, my cousin had fallen hard for Sonny. His sly, bad-boy charm worked.

"Is he gone?"

Bree's question startled me.

"Tell me what you saw in him," I demanded.

"Sonny? Lord, I don't hardly remember."

"You remember Dillon McBride? He was cute, had a good job, and had the hugest crush on you . . . but you looked right through him and winked at Sonny."

Bree laughed. "Dillon. Wow. Blast from the past." She sighed. "Dillon just didn't have an edge."

"Edge is overrated."

She elbowed me. "Are you kidding? Didn't you just pass over a gorgeous, steady, loyal hunk of a man in favor of a bad boy?"

"Touché." I cut my eyes in her direction. "So you think Cal McCormack is gorgeous?"

A blazing blush burned her cheeks. I couldn't believe Bree, my brash and rowdy cousin, was blushing over a boy. "Oh, hush. You know what I mean."

"Mmm-hmm." It was true. Cal was a mighty fine man. But I had never realized Bree had noticed.

Curious.

"Well, I was crazy when I fell for Sonny. But at least I got Alice out of the deal. And now maybe she'll get a little something to make her life better, too."

I understood where Bree was coming from, and I didn't like the idea of Sonny bullying his way out of child support, but I couldn't help wondering whether the price would prove too dear.

# chapter 7

"Are you sure?"

Cal sighed. "Dang it, Tally. Of course I'm sure. This is my job, and I do it pretty well."

"Don't get testy, Cal. I'm just askin'."

"And I'm just sayin'." Cal gave me a hard look. "Let's not forget that I'm doing you a monumental favor by doing this walk-through with you. It's not exactly legit."

"Oh, come on. The scene's been cleared. The only reason they haven't started up the ride again is that everyone's too creeped out by what happened."

"Right. We're not doing anything illegal here, but it's a little out of the ordinary for me to give the prime suspect's cousin a guided tour of the crime scene the day after a murder."

He stood near the mini train track that ran through

the saloon display in the haunted rodeo, his feet planted on a red X taped on the floor. "So like I was saying, the angle isn't right for me," he said, "because I'm taller, but the crime scene folks said that based on the angle and location of the entry wound, Kristen was crouched down low in the train car and the shooter was standing here, aiming down toward her." He illustrated his words by extending his arm, his thumb and forefinger cocked like a gun.

"Wait. Back up. What do you mean, you're taller? Taller than what?"

"Taller than Bree."

"Taller than Bree? Or taller than the killer?"

Cal took a careful step back, as though he were easing off a land mine, and then he turned to face me. "All they really know is the angle of entry for the bullet. So you can draw a line, at an angle, back from where Kristen was located when she was killed. Exactly how far back the killer was depends on how tall the shooter was."

Geometry was never my forte, but even I could see the flaw in this logic. "So they only put that mark on the floor right there because they assumed the shooter was Bree's height?"

Cal frowned. "Well, sort of."

"There's no 'sort of' about it. If the shooter was as tall as you are, he wouldn't have been standing on that X. You just said so yourself."

He pulled his hat from his head and ran his fingers through his hair. "Right, but even if the killer was, say, six-four or six-five, that would mean he was standing back a few feet. Not over there by the saloon doors like Bree said."

"Are you sure?"

His chin dropped to his chest in defeat.

"Look, I want to believe Bree, too. Honest. We did find a slug back behind Old Cletus over there"—Cal gestured toward the zombie cowboy blocking the saloon doors—"which backs up part of Bree's story. But I asked the techs if it was possible the person who shot Kristen was standing by the saloon doors. They said, if that were true, the shooter would have been eight feet tall. I've known some pretty tall Texans in my day, but no one that tall."

I walked over to the saloon doors and sidled up to the mannequin dressed as a zombie cowboy. Up close, I could see the layer of grime streaking his leering greenish-gray face, and a bright white streak across the side of his hat where Bree's bullet had grazed him.

I tipped back my head and tried to figure out where the eight-foot man's hand would have been. "So the gun would have been right about where?"

Cal joined me. He reached up and tapped the top of the artificial doorframe. "About here."

I stepped back into the center of the room and let my eyes rest on the place he indicated. Then I looked down. And then I looked up.

Right up the frilly, glittery skirt of the saloon girl perched above the door.

I pointed at her. "What about there? What if the shooter had been up on that little balcony? Where the saloon girl is?"

He looked up to where I was pointing. Without warning, he jerked back his head, then doubled over in pain.

"Cal!" I rushed the few steps to his side and wrapped my arm around his shoulders to support him. "Are you okay?"

He straightened, rubbing his right eye. "I'm fine. Just got something in my eye."

I pried his hand away from his face. "Here, let me look."

The light inside the ride cast amber shadows across his strong features. Even in that anemic glow, though, I could see the flash of red glitter dotting his cheekbone.

"Hold still," I commanded. I dabbed my forefinger with my tongue and carefully brushed the glitter away.

"Sorry," I said. "Wiley said the dancer drops that glitter all the time. I should have warned you."

He stepped out of my reach, lifting his hand to wipe moisture from his eye. "I'm fine," he muttered.

He sniffed and then lifted his gaze to the saloon girl's balcony. He frowned. "That's too high," he said.

"It's too high if Kristen was crouching in the bottom of the car, but what if she was sitting or standing in the car?"

He looked from the balcony to the tracks and back again. "Maybe," he conceded.

I pulled my purse from my shoulder and dug around for a ballpoint pen, dropped the purse to the ground, hustled over to the train, and stepped into the car. I suppressed a shudder at the thought I was standing on the spot where Kristen died, and crouched down to the floor. "I'm about Kristen's size," I said.

Without me asking, Cal walked back to the X on the floor, bent his knees a bit, and lifted his arm as though he were shooting at my head. Carefully, I brought the pen to my forehead, trying to match the angle of the bullet from Cal's imaginary gun.

He stepped forward, gently shifted the pen in my hand to correct the angle.

Then, holding the pen steady, I climbed onto the car's seat.

Cal's long legs made short work of clambering into the next car back and then into the seat beside me. He hunkered down on the seat so his face was nestled close to mine. I could feel his warm breath stirring the wisps of hair at my temple. I shivered.

"No," he said finally. "Still not right."

His hand cupped my elbow and, with just a little pressure, he urged me to stand. I rose to my feet, shaky.

His large fingers rested on the back of my neck, subtly adjusting the angle of my head. My head tipped back, chin raised. The stance was proud, defiant. And my eyes were fixed firmly on the dancing girl.

"There," he said softly. "The angle matches."

I opened my fingers, letting the pen drop to the metal floor of the car with a hollow rattle. "The shooter was on the balcony," I said.

I shivered again as Cal pulled away from me, as cool air filled the space between us.

"Maybe," he said.

"Right," I said. "Either the shooter was on the balcony, and Kristen was standing in the car looking up at him—"

"Or," Cal said, "the shooter was in the middle of the floor—right where Bree was standing when we found her—and Kristen was cowering in fear."

"How can we tell what happened?"

He set his hands on my upper arms, shifting me to the side so he could get past. Once again, he crossed the floor to the saloon doors. I followed.

We both edged around the zombie, pushing aside the swinging doors to peer at the back of the facade.

Between the fake saloon wall and the real wall of the attraction, there was a gap of about four feet. Looking along the real wall, I could make out the faint glow of sunlight around two separate doors to the outside, probably emergency exits, though they weren't marked.

"Someone else could have been in here," I said. "They could have shot Kristen and slipped through one of those doors."

Cal nodded once, a tight gesture. "Yep. I'll give you that. If someone got up to the balcony and back down. But that's a mighty big 'if.'"

I wedged in farther behind the cowboy zombie and looked up. Lights were set in the real wall just above the height of the saloon door opening. Beyond the lights, there was nothing but metal braces and cobwebs.

Two-inch pipes, spaced about six feet apart, supported the back of the saloon facade. About fifteen feet up, the pipes were joined by horizontal lengths of slightly narrower pipe.

Directly above our heads, light shone through the

opening for the balcony. On the backside, there was no lip or ledge from the balcony.

I ducked back to the front of the facade and studied the fake balcony a bit closer.

The dancer sat on a ledge no more than eighteen inches deep.

There wasn't much room to either side of her, and even less behind her.

I looked at Cal questioningly.

"No way," he said.

"There's enough room for a person up there," I insisted.

"Barely. And how would a person get up there? There isn't enough room back behind that facade for a ladder."

"Maybe someone put a ladder up on the front side."

"So where did the ladder go? Bree didn't mention seeing any ladder, much less seeing someone climb down and haul a ladder away with them. And you and I got inside here within five minutes of the first shot being fired. A single person, moving fast, could have gotten out one of those emergency doors. But I don't buy someone dismantling a ladder from out here, squeezing it around the mannequin, working it through all those pipes and struts behind the facade, and getting out an emergency door before we came in."

He shook his head.

"I'm sorry, Tally. As much as I want to believe her, Bree's story just doesn't add up. And all the physical evidence points to her being in here alone with Kristen when she was killed."

# *chapter 8*

Some folks might think it strange that, with my life lying in ruins at my feet, I would bother to keep a hair appointment. But those folks wouldn't be from Dalliance. Frankly, personal crisis is no excuse for dark roots.

Here, the bond between hairdresser and lady ranks right up there with that between doctor and patient, lawyer and client, priest and penitent. A sacred trust is forged in the shampoo bowl and tempered by countless blow-outs, a trust that cannot be broken. That trust kept me loyal to Karla Faye Hoffstead of the Hair Apparent Salon for two and a half decades. During my marriage to Wayne Jones, I could have gone to fancier salons—in fact, Wayne begged me to go mingle with the high-class ladies at the day spas that cropped up along FM 410—but I'd stayed true to Karla Faye.

Everything about the Hair Apparent—the scuffed linoleum floors, the acrid scent of perm solution and overheated plastic, and the chaos of women shouting to be heard above hair dryers and running water—felt familiar, comfortable.

About an hour after I left Cal McCormack outside the haunted rodeo ride, I took my seat in Karla Faye's chair and gripped the arms as she pumped the foot pedal to raise me up to a more convenient level. She whipped one of her leopard-print capes around my shoulders and began segregating and studying hanks of my hair with a critical eye.

"Unh, unh, unh," she muttered. "Tally, don't you ever deep condition your hair? I could use these ends for kindling."

I grimaced. "I know. It's pitiful. But I've had a lot on my mind."

Karla Faye met my gaze in the mirror. "Lordy, don't I know it? The shop's been buzzing all day about the murder."

"What are people saying?" The Hair Apparent clientele was a microcosm of Dalliance. If you wanted to see which way the wind of public opinion was blowing, Karla Faye could give you a pretty accurate forecast.

She busied herself parting and reparting my hair with a rat-tail comb, inspecting my roots as she went. "Mmm. Well, I'd say folks are split about seventy-thirty that Bree did it." She shrugged. "But a hundred percent of 'em think Kristen had it coming."

I half turned in the chair, trying to look her in the face, but she grasped my shoulders in her strikingly strong hands and held me in place. "Unless you want to lose an eye, you need to stay still." She waved the comb with its stiletto-like handle for emphasis.

"Sorry."

"Come on, let's get you shampooed." Karla Faye helped me out of the chair and led me over to the shampoo bowl.

"So, why do people think Kristen deserved to be killed?" I asked.

Karla Faye snorted. "Lord only knows what all that uppity woman had going on. That woman was colder than a witch's tit."

"Karla Faye!"

She rolled her eyes. "Oh, I know. I shouldn't speak ill of the dead." She paused while she doused my hair with lukewarm water. As hot as it was outside, the water felt deliciously cool against my scalp.

"Anyway," she continued, squirting some citrusy-smelling shampoo into her hand, "you know what that woman was doing?"

I sighed. Karla Faye always had the juiciest information, and she loved to share it, but she took her own sweet time doing it. She'd milk a bit of gossip harder than a dried-up milch cow. She began working the shampoo through my hair, her fingers massaging in circular motions that seemed to keep time with the cadence of her chatter.

"Well, Shelley Alrecht came in to get her highlights touched up for the big karaoke contest at the fair. And she told me that she heard from Cookie Milhone—you know Cookie? She runs that new flower shop over in

Lantana Plaza? And she's the hospitality chair for the League of Methodist Ladies?"

I did, indeed, know Cookie Milhone. Cookie had eaten chicken cordon bleu at my dining table and sipped pinot grigio by my pool . . . and, as I learned during my divorce proceedings, diddled my ex-husband. Before he was my ex.

"Well," Karla Faye continued, "Cookie Milhone told Shelley that Kristen Ver Steeg was going to disqualify Dani Carberry from the Rodeo Queen Pageant."

I was grateful for the lull in conversation as Karla Faye rinsed me. It gave me a chance to work through that big ol' clump of information. I didn't know the Carberrys very well, but Finn worked with Mike Carberry at the *Dalliance News-Letter*. Mike and his wife, Eloise, had a daughter who was just about Alice's age. In fact, I seemed to recall that Alice and Dani Carberry were in the same class until Alice started skipping grades.

The morning Kristen was killed, Cal was on his way to a meeting of the pageant judges, a meeting Kristen had called to deal with a problem. Maybe that problem had been Dani Carberry. And if that was so, it might explain why Kristen had recused herself from mediating the dispute between Eloise Carberry and Tucker Gentry over Tucker's ice cream entry. But I'd be the first to admit I was reaching here.

And Eloise Carberry wasn't really the type to patronize the Hair Apparent, so I couldn't imagine why Karla Faye and the rest of the girls would get so out of whack about Dani being disqualified from the pageant, anyway. Why would the Hair Apparent tribe choose sides at all in a battle between two women from the Botox and designer shoes crowd?

Karla Faye wrapped a towel around my head and helped me back to my feet.

"Why would Dani be disqualified?" I asked.

She spun around on her spiky heels. I loved her to pieces, but Karla Faye always dressed like an extra in *Grease*. That day, she was decked out in white skinny jeans, a tight purple tank top, wide white patent leather belt, and purple sparkly high-heeled sandals, her orange-painted toenails peeping out like teeny tiny kumquats. I hesitated to think what her veins were like, after thirty-odd years of ten-hour days, on her feet, in totally ridiculous shoes. But Karla Faye was a firm believer in suffering for beauty.

"Shelley didn't have all the details, but I'm guessing it's because of the wig."

"You lost me."

"Dani's wig," she said again, as if that made everything clear.

"Why would Dani wear a wig? Bad dye job?"

She clasped her hand to her breast in shock. "Lord, haven't you heard?"

"For the love of God, Karla Faye . . . heard what? Let's just assume I've been living under a rock for the past year and don't have any idea what you're talking about."

I plopped down in the chair at Karla Faye's station. I was starting to get a little irked.

"Oh, honey, Dani Carberry has the cancer." She whispered "the cancer" as if it were a dirty word.

"What?" How on earth had I missed that? I mean, Finn and Mike Carberry worked together.

Karla Faye nodded solemnly. "Yeah, poor kid."

"What kind of cancer?"

"Oh, I'm sure I don't know. But something bad. She's been getting treatments all summer and her hair all fell out. She's a flag corps cadet at the high school, and the other flag girls did that thing where you cut off your hair and send it to some place to make wigs for girls with cancer. I had about a half dozen in here one day a few weeks ago, all crying like babies while I hacked off their ponytails and wrapped 'em up in tinfoil. They walked out of here with a big ol' bag of hair."

"Wow, that's horrible. Poor Eloise."

Karla Faye combed out my hair and began carving off little sections that she twisted up and pinned on my head.

"That little girl has been so brave," she said. "The flag girls said Dani was going to enter the Rodeo Queen Pageant to raise awareness about cancer and how bad it is. And they're already talking about how she's a lock for homecoming queen. Can you imagine getting up on a stage and smiling and waving when you're wearing someone else's hair on your head?"

I shook my head. Honestly, it was pretty moving.

"And then that awful Kristen woman comes along and plans to crush her dreams, just like that"—she snapped her fingers. "What kind of horrible, heartless person tells a little girl with cancer that she has to walk that pageant all bald-headed?"

I frowned. "Wait. Are you sure that's what happened? I mean, do you know that she was going to disqualify Dani and that the wig was the reason?"

Karla Faye stiffened. "Well, no. But Shelley said that Cookie is on the panel of judges for the pageant, and Kristen called her and said they had a problem with Dani. I mean, what else could it be?"

An excellent question. And one I surely intended to answer. Even if it meant standing face-to-face with Cookie Milhone.

By the time Karla Faye was done snipping and styling my chestnut hair into something approaching a hairdo, I was itching to get out of the Hair Apparent and find out more about Dani Carberry's alleged expulsion from the Rodeo Queen Pageant.

Finn was expecting me at his house for dinner before the two of us spent the evening going through the boxes stashed in his mother's attic.

Finn had moved back to Dalliance to take care of his widowed mother after her second major stroke. Over the summer, she'd begun having mini strokes, what the doctors called transient ischemic attacks, on an increasingly regular basis. It meant she might suffer another massive stroke, and she needed more constant monitoring of her situation. As a result, Finn bit the bullet and moved his mama into a nursing home in July.

Ever since, he'd been rattling around the house in which he'd grown up, alone with the ghosts of his departed father and the brother who died too young.

The time had finally come to go through the boxes of his brother's high school football paraphernalia, his dad's hunting trophies, and his mom's accumulation of tchotchkes. As a dutiful girlfriend, I got to help.

When I left the Hair Apparent, I had about a half hour before I was supposed to be at Finn's. I pointed my craptastic van away from Dalliance proper and headed toward FM 410, Lantana Plaza, and the Lilting Bloom.

I was in luck. Cookie Milhone, the owner of Dalliance's newest florist, was in the store that afternoon.

It's a well-established fact that you're either born a Texan or you're not. The state is wedded with your flesh and bone at birth, as tough to extract as the petroleum in north Texas's rich shale bed.

I had a few friends who skedaddled north the second they could, to places like Chicago and Boston and even Seattle. They still came back to Dalliance with big hair, Botox, and more twang than a truck full of banjos.

Cookie Milhone had left Dalliance after high school, gone off to some college in California where they offer classes on the philosophy of surfing and postfeminist psychoanalysis for St. Bernards. She returned to Texas five years later with the zeal of the born again, wearing plenty of rhinestones and dropping y'alls all over the place.

Cookie looked like a china doll. She stood all of five-foot-nothing, with buttercup hair set in a profusion of lacquered barrel curls, lips a glossy poppy red, and lily-white skin. It was her eyes, though, that made her look like a doll: Thick black lashes fringed her startling cornflower eyes, and she blinked seldom and slowly.

"Hey, shug," she drawled, accent as thick and sweet as cane syrup. "Can I help you?"

"Hi, Cookie."

She blinked once, eyes vacant.

"Tally," I prompted. "Tally Jones."

She blinked again, and a blinding smile spread across her face. "Oh, Tally!" *Buh-link.* "I haven't seen you since—well, since the divorce." She whispered that last, even though we were the only two souls in the store. And even though her name was in boldface type in paragraph 43 of my divorce decree, so it wasn't exactly a secret between us.

Lord a'mighty.

"It's been a while," I conceded.

*Buh-link.*

"A little birdie told me there's a new man in your life," she said, her lips pursing in a semblance of a smile.

*Little birdie.* Right. More like a flock of grackles. Everyone in Dalliance had something to say about my renewed relationship with Finn Harper.

Cookie gave me a quick once-over. "Finn Harper's quite a catch," she said.

*Buh-link.*

Suddenly, Cookie's dead eyes made me think less of a baby doll and more of a shark, cruising the water for fresh meat. And I didn't fancy chumming the waters with any more talk of my handsome, accomplished significant other.

"Nice store," I said.

Cookie cocked her head and her flat blue eyes rolled like marbles in her head as she looked around the store, seeming to see it for the first time. "Thanks," she said. "I was so bored, you know. And I always liked flowers."

I felt a twinge of resentment that this woman could run a business as a hobby, pumping in all the cash she needed to keep the storefront tidy, the case filled with flowers, the most lovely vases on display. Meanwhile, my whole family worked our fingers to the bone to keep the vertical batch freezers churning one more day at the A-la-mode.

"Are you looking for something special?" Cookie said. "We just got in some exquisite dahlias. Vibrant orange centers with gold tracing along the edge of the petals."

"Sounds beautiful," I said. "But I wanted to send something to Kristen Ver Steeg's law office. Express my condolences. I don't know if she has family in the area."

Cookie blinked twice, quickly. I had her attention now.

"Kristen didn't have family here," she said. "I think she was from down near Galveston, but I got the impression she didn't have any family at all, really." She sighed. "So sad."

"It certainly is. She contributed so much to the community. Involved with the fair and all."

She chuckled low in her throat. "I'm not sure she was making many friends that way."

"Really?" I put on my best wide-eyed innocent face. "But she gave so much of her time, was taking her commitment to the job so seriously."

Cookie clicked her tongue against her teeth. "Maybe a little too seriously," she said.

"What do you mean?"

"Eloise has been chair of the pageant committee for years, of course. The only reason she's not this year is because Dani's competing. Conflict of interest, you know."

I nodded. That made sense.

"Eloise was trying to figure out who should take her place this year, and then she went to a Pampered Chef party at Kristen's house. Saw all of Kristen's pageant crowns. She even had a big one for Miss American Pride 2001. Eloise figured Kristen would give the event some added legitimacy, and that way, when Dani won, it would be an even bigger deal. But Kristen was just supposed to be a placeholder, you know. I told Eloise it was a mistake. Kristen would take the job way too seriously. She was a lawyer, you know," Cookie said, as though that explained everything.

When I just stared blankly at her, she huffed impatiently. "She was a bit of a stickler for the rules. Had a real stick up her you-know-what. And that didn't sit well with everyone, if you get my drift."

I didn't get her drift at all. First, as a fellow rule-stickler, I didn't appreciate the mental picture Cookie was painting. Second, in my experience, lawyers were more interested in getting *around* rules than in actually following them.

"Following the rules is usually a good thing, right?" I said, a little defensively.

"Well, the Lantana Round-Up has rules, but not all rules are created equal, you know? Some matter more than others. Kristen was getting hung up on some of the little details that were on the books but never meant to be enforced. She was all trees, no forest."

"Could you give me a for-example?"

Cookie leaned up on her tiptoes to peek over my shoulder, make sure we were alone.

"It wasn't official or anything, but she was calling a meeting of the pageant judges just yesterday. Right before she died. You didn't hear this from me, but she said was going to move to disqualify Dani Carberry from the competition because of a rules infraction."

I gasped, trying to sound suitably shocked. "Dani Carberry? Isn't she on the honor roll? What kind of rule could she have broken?"

Cookie shrugged. "I don't know. There's a huge long list of rules for the pageant. Age and residence requirements, morals clauses, academic standards. But Kristen was pretty fixated on the artifice rules."

"The what?"

"The artifice rules," Cookie repeated slowly, as if I were a little dense. "You know, what sorts of artificial beauty enhancers you can and cannot use. Kristen made sure we all had a copy of the lists."

"There are lists?"

I didn't mean to repeat everything Cookie said, but I was trying to wrap my brain around what she was saying.

"Sure. Lists of things you can use, and things that are strictly off-limits. Spray tans are okay. Mascara, yes, false eyelashes, no. Highlights, yes, perms, relaxers, and all-over color, no." She leaned forward. "Weird thing was Kristen was an alum of the glitz pageant circuit. Anything goes in the glitz pageants—fake hair, false eyelashes, airbrushing away freckles, flippers, you name it."

"Flippers?"

"Partial dentures to hide missing baby teeth."

"Oh." Of course. Why didn't I think of that? "But why is that weird?"

"Well, the good Lord only knows what kind of smoke and mirrors Kristen used to win her crowns. Some of the rodeo pageant girls are, uh, a little plain . . . to put it delicately. Why would she want to deny them the chance to look their best?"

I didn't know Dani Carberry well at all, but I'd seen her a time or two. She wasn't even a tiny bit plain. "Dani's a gorgeous girl. What kind of artifice could she possibly want that wouldn't be allowed in the rules?"

Cookie's eyes narrowed and she pursed her lips. "Only one thing I can think of."

"The wig?"

She crooked an eyebrow in response.

"But Kristen never said that was the problem, right? I mean, she never told you that Dani's wig would disqualify her?"

Cookie shook her head, her starched curls dancing around her delicate chin. "No. In fact, the rules don't specifically say wigs are illegal. But hair weaves are definitely not allowed, and wigs aren't on the list of acceptable enhancements. And, honestly, Dani's such a wonderful girl. What else could it have been?"

"Maybe Dani got into trouble recently? Something she managed to keep quiet."

Cookie tipped her head back and gave me a smug look. "I surely don't think so. I'll have you know that Eloise Carberry and I are very close. We're both on the board of the League of Methodist Ladies. As soon as Kristen called the meeting, I contacted Eloise. She was as shocked as I was at the allegation Dani had done something improper."

And there was no way Dani could have done any-thing wrong without her mother knowing about it.

Ha.

# chapter 9

I shoved a tissue-wrapped bouquet of miniature sunflowers in Finn's face. "Why didn't you tell me Dani Carberry has cancer?"

"What?" He took the flowers and stood aside to let me into his foyer. He led me back to the kitchen, where he'd been setting out sandwich fixings for our supper, and put the flowers in a cobalt glass pitcher. A basket of potato chips and two sweating glasses of iced tea were already laid out on the dining table.

"You heard me, Finn," I said, leaning against the counter to watch him cook. "I found out today that Mike's daughter has cancer. You work with the guy. Surely the topic came up at some point."

Finn paused in the act of peeling the foil from a container of leftover barbecue. Everyone and his uncle were doing dress rehearsals for the fair's big BBQ cook-off, so the whole town was on an all-barbecue diet for the week. At Erma's Fry by Night, they even had a brisket quiche on the specials board.

"He mentioned she had a little cancer, but it was no big deal."

I smacked my forehead with my palm. "No big deal? Cancer, Finn. Cancer's always a big deal."

He sighed. "It didn't sound like a big deal. Mike mentioned last spring, before you and I started dating, that Dani had a little skin cancer removed from her shoulder. Dani was mad because her prom dress was backless and Mike wouldn't let her wait until after the dance to have the procedure, so she had a Band-Aid showing in her prom pictures. And Mike was mad because he found out Eloise had been letting Dani go to a tanning salon. And Eloise was mad because, between you and me, I think Eloise is always mad."

"That's it? He just mentioned it once? Didn't you ask how she was doing?"

He popped the container of pulled pork in the microwave and started it reheating. "Never thought of it again. We live in Texas, Tally. No stinkin' ozone layer is going to protect us from the sun's harmful rays. My mom had moles whacked off every year, no big deal. Besides, Mike brought it up in the context of 'our house is pretty tense these days.' He didn't seem particularly worried, so I didn't think it was anything serious."

"Well, apparently it is."

Finn pulled two kaiser rolls from a bakery bag, plopped them on a couple of plates, and handed one to me. He squinted his eyes and tilted his head, skeptical. "I saw Dani at the fairgrounds the other night. She looked fine."

"She's in chemo. She's lost all her hair."

"Naw . . . she has hair down to her shoulder blades." He reached around to tap his own back to demonstrate how long her hair was.

"It's a wig," I insisted.

"Really? Huh. Well, I'm telling you, Mike hasn't said a word." The microwave beeped and he clicked open the door to give the barbecue a stir. "But . . ."

"But what?"

He shrugged. "The other night when I was at the Parlay Inn asking around about Sonny and his friend, I was talking with Mike. I don't even remember how it came up, but he started going on about Dani being all grown up, entering this pageant, looking at college, starting to spread her wings, and he . . . well, he teared up."

"You didn't mention that before."

His eyebrows shot up. "I didn't mention that I found a penny on the way into the bar, either. Or that I bought a new three-pack of boxers."

"Don't be a smart aleck. Mike getting all choked up over his daughter is a whole different thing."

"I didn't think it was particularly relevant. At the time, I figured he was just maudlin from too many gin and tonics, thinking about where the time went, how his gap-toothed little girl in pigtails could be a grown woman. In retrospect, he might have been upset because she's sick. But I still don't see what that has to do with anything."

I felt a pang of contrition. After all, Finn was doing

a lot of legwork for me and Bree, and I did sound as if I was accusing him of incompetence. "Sorry. I don't know if I would have thought anything of it before today, either."

The microwave dinged again, and I held out my plate so Finn could pile barbecue on my bun. We made our way over to the dinette table and set our plates on his mama's burgundy quilted place mats.

"Today, though, Karla Faye told me that Kristen was disqualifying Dani from the pageant."

Finn pointed at my head with his fork. "Your hair looks nice, by the way. Cutting a little shorter brings out your curls."

A wave of pleasure washed through me. I patted my hair self-consciously. "Thanks. She did a nice job."

He winked at me, and a wave of something a lot more wicked washed through me.

"Oh, hush," I muttered. "Eat."

He picked up his sandwich and took a healthy bite.

"Why disqualify her?" he asked around a mouthful of barbecue.

"Mmm. No one is really sure, but the speculation is that it might be against pageant rules to wear a wig. Anyway, I got to thinking. If my daughter was sick and maybe dying and she wanted to win a pageant and someone told her she couldn't even compete, I'd be mighty angry."

Finn narrowed his eyes thoughtfully while he finished chewing. "Did Mike even know about the disqualification?"

"Yep. I went out to the Lilting Bloom and talked to

Cookie Milhone. She's on the board of the League of
Methodist Ladies with Eloise Carberry, and she's on
the judging panel for the Rodeo Queen Pageant."

Finn shook his head in mock hurt. "I thought you
brought me flowers because you care. And now I find
out it was just cover for your snooping."

I let my lips curl in a coy smile. "Poor baby. I'll
make it up to you."

"Tallulah Jones. You vixen."

We both busted up laughing.

"The point I'm trying to make, if you'd keep your
mind out of the gutter, is that Cookie Milhone got a
call from Kristen about needing to get the judges together to talk about Dani. And then Cookie, being a
good friend, called Eloise and gave her a heads-up."

"Hmm. But I really can't see Mike Carberry as a killer. Besides, the morning Kristen was killed, we had a
staff meeting at the paper. Mike was sitting right next
to me when the call about shots fired came over the
police scanner. He couldn't have done it."

"I wasn't thinking of Mike. I was thinking of Eloise."

Finn popped a chip in his mouth. "Interesting. Eloise
is kind of a bitch."

"Finn!"

He laughed darkly. "She is. Ask anyone. You know,
she got a waitress at the Prickly Pear Café fired for
dropping a bottle of hot sauce on her lap. It was an
accident, and the bottle wasn't even open. But she told
the manager that he was lucky she didn't sue and
she'd never come back to the restaurant again unless
he fired the poor kid."

"Wow."

"But," he continued, "it's a long way from getting a waitress fired to killing a lawyer."

"I don't know. It's just a matter of degree. I hadn't heard the story about the waitress, but I know she went after Tucker Gentry like a terminator robot because he made a snide remark about her cooking skills. It's a pattern, right? Someone gets in her way, she does what it takes to destroy them."

Finn grimaced and shook his head. "I don't know, Tally."

"She can shoot, too. Remember last year there was the brouhaha about the Methodist Ladies hosting that fund-raiser with the marksmanship contest? Some people didn't think that was the most appropriate way to raise money for wounded veterans. But Eloise won that contest."

Finn looked skeptical.

"She was a gymnast in high school, wasn't she?"

He nodded. "Went to college on scholarship. Almost made the Olympic team."

"So she maybe could have pulled herself up to the balcony where the saloon girl was sitting. She has the upper body strength."

"Had," Finn corrected.

"She's still real fit," I insisted. "I bet she still has some moves."

"Look, I'm not saying she didn't do it," Finn said. "I'm just saying you need a lot more to go on if you think you're going to shift the blame from Bree to Eloise."

"I know. Will you help me get it?"

Finn's expression grew serious. He reached out to take my hand. "You know I'd do anything for you."

A warm stillness came over me, as if Finn and I were in a bubble of quiet apart from all the crazy in our lives.

Finn liked to tease, and I liked to laugh, so our relationship was mostly pretty lighthearted. Lord knows, we needed a little light in our lives to help us forget all the sorrow and fear: Finn's mom out at the Garrity Arms Nursing Home, slipping further and further away from us with every tiny pinpoint stroke. The A-la-mode, where every step forward seemed dogged by two steps back. Alice's pain over her daddy. Bree's fear of being arrested.

But in that solemn moment, I didn't just forget about those things . . . they simply ceased to exist. The entire universe was me, Finn, and the yearning heat between us.

He tightened his grip on my hand, his eyes burning into me. "You know, right?"

I opened my mouth, but no words would come. I nodded.

He pushed away from the table and gently tugged me to my feet. One step brought him up against me. His gentle kiss on my lips was a benediction.

Walking backward, his eyes never leaving mine, he led me to the stairs, and together we climbed to his room. Everything else—Bree, Alice, the murder—it would have to wait.

# chapter 10

I've heard tell that the Eskimos have thirty different words for *white*. In Texas, we reserve that granularity of description for our summer heat. You'd think Texans would simply be used to hot, would suck it up and go about their business. But we're the biggest wusses in the world when the mercury inches into the triple digits.

That particular summer strained our collective ability to describe heat. We stretched every metaphor to the breaking point, and still we couldn't quite capture the ungodly, never-ending, smothering, oppressive, makes-you-want-to-turn-your-own-skin-inside-out quality of the weather that August.

It kept the daytime crowds at the fair thin and listless, but it meant good business at the A-la-mode.

After a long but enjoyable night with Finn, I stood

shoulder to shoulder beside Kyle Mason, both of us dipping cones until our hands cramped, trying to keep the fairgoers from expiring.

During a brief lull just before lunch, I caught Kyle watching me out of the corner of his eye. His head was tipped down so his dark mop of hair—this silly-looking combed-forward bowl cut that all the teen boys seemed to be wearing—fell nearly to the tip of his nose, but I could still see the lines of worry around his mouth.

When he met my gaze, he tossed his head, flipping his hair back in a practiced move that was just a bit too self-conscious to be genuinely cool.

"Is Alice okay?" he asked.

I sighed. "I think so. Or at least, she will be. She's a tough girl. She'll get through this."

He picked at his thumbnail with his teeth. I made a mental note to have him use the hand sanitizer liberally before serving any more customers.

"CnnnItllsmtg?" he muttered.

"Enunciate, Kyle. Learn to use your words," I teased.

"Can I tell you something?" he repeated, shifting his weight from one foot to the other.

The tremor of emotion in his voice made me get real serious real fast. Kyle was a surly teenage boy with a significant juvie record. He did not emote unless something was wrong.

"Of course. You can tell me anything," I soothed.

*Please don't let Alice be pregnant, please don't let Alice be pregnant, please don't let Alice be pregnant . . .*

"The other night, after Alice found out her dad was back in town, I let her borrow the Bonnie."

Our intellectual prodigy, Alice, had to take her driver's test three times before she passed. She still had a limited learner's permit, which meant she wasn't legally allowed to drive without someone twenty-one or over in the front seat with her. In other words, she wasn't supposed to be tooling around Dalliance in Kyle's Bonneville.

On the one hand, I didn't want to condone this behavior. On the other hand, I didn't want to spook Kyle. I got the feeling there was more to this story yet to come.

"Huh," I hedged. "Know where she went?"

He shook his head, shaggy hair flopping back and forth. "After the midway closed down, I was stuck here. I called her like ten times, but she didn't answer. Finally, she showed up after midnight. Wouldn't tell me where she'd been."

I had this mental image of Kyle just sitting out behind the A-la-mode booth, alone with his thoughts, patiently waiting for Alice to come back with his car. He hadn't called any of his friends, or his parents, or us . . . he'd just waited for her. He might be a big dork with a rap sheet, but I got why Alice liked him so much.

"I'm worried about her," Kyle said, raising his head to look me square in the eye. "I don't know how to help her."

I took a risk and looped my arm around his shoulders, pulling him into a reluctant hug. "I don't know, either. We just have to be patient. I think you can do that."

His body spasmed a bit, something I took for a laugh. "Guess so. Not like I got anyplace else to go."

I let him pull free. "Oh, Kyle, that's not true. I'm happy you and Alice have each other, but you shouldn't stay together just because you don't feel like you have other options. You always have other options."

His shoulders jerked up to his ears. I spoke "teenager" fluently enough to know he didn't agree.

"You do. I know you struggled in school, but that's because you were bored. You're not stupid. Heck, if you were stupid, Alice wouldn't waste her time with you. If you want to learn a trade, or go on to school, or whatever, you can do it. You really do have options."

"I guess."

By that point, the boy's ears were as red as my brandied cherry sauce. Thankfully, we were saved from further awkward bonding by a new onslaught of customers.

"Kyle," I snapped as he reached for a sugar cone, "sanitize first, my friend."

He huffed a melodramatic sigh, but did as he was bid. We were back in familiar territory, and I smiled softly at the return to normalcy.

"Tally Jones, I have a bone to pick with you."

*Bye-bye, smile.*

Eloise Carberry bore down on the A-la-mode booth like a semi hurtling down a steep grade. She still had a gymnast's build, slender and straight. Not that you could make out much of a figure beneath her no-nonsense tan chinos and her embroidered chambray shirt. Her frosted brown hair was set in face-framing layers sprayed into fierce submission, much like a mideighties Mary Lou Retton. Eloise was a handsome woman, might have been on the homecoming court, but would never have been queen. She ruled the League of Methodist Ladies with dictatorial efficiency, but she'd never crack into the Junior League set. There was just something a little too practical about her. A little too workaday. A little too matronly.

But that very no-nonsense quality made her seem bigger than she was. And when I found myself in the crosshairs of her thin-lipped frown, I took a step back.

"Hiya, Eloise. Enjoying the fair?"

"It's too hot to enjoy anything." Something about the way she said it made it seem as if the weather were her own personal cross to bear.

"Oh. Sorry to hear that."

"Tally, we need to talk. Tucker Gentry competing in the ice cream category is an absolute travesty. You and I both know he stole that flavor profile from you. Why, the man should be disqualified from all the edibles contests."

Given the number of second-place ribbons Eloise took home the year before, I could just imagine how anxious she was to have her biggest competition disqualified from the events.

"Now, Eloise, I trust Garrett's judgment."

She snorted. "Letting Garrett Simms make that call," she huffed. "That's the fox guarding the henhouse if ever I saw it."

"I'm not sure I follow," I said. In fact, I was pretty certain she was using the idiom all wrong.

"They're both, you know . . ." She leaned in close, but didn't bother to drop her tone a lick. "Perverts."

I smothered a sigh. While I had managed to remain in the dark until the year before, Garrett Simms's preference for men was one of the most unsecret secrets in all of Dalliance. It didn't bother his wife any, and as long as the two of them were happy with the arrangement, most folks just let them be.

But Tucker Gentry was a youth pastor at a very conservative church. An allegation that he was gay, whether it was true or not, could do him some serious damage.

I stepped off to the side of the counter, pulling Eloise as far from my line of customers as I could. "Eloise," I hissed, "it's not like gay people all have some secret handshake. Even if Tucker is gay, there's no reason to think that Garrett would show him any favoritism."

"Oh, he's not . . . well, that," Eloise said. "He's just a pervert. Spends all his time with girls young enough to be his daughters."

"He's a youth pastor. It's his job."

Eloise crossed her arms and set her lips in a mutinous frown. "Exactly."

"You're not making any sense. Are you suggesting that everyone who chooses to work with kids has an unnatural attraction to them?"

"Not at all. But that man is creepy."

Now we were getting to the heart of the matter. It wasn't that poor Tucker had done anything at all. He was just odd. And for Eloise, "odd" had to be put into some sort of box. Apparently she'd chosen "pervert" for Tucker.

"Creepy isn't a crime. And even if it was, Tucker being creepy doesn't put him in the same boat with Garrett, who isn't creepy at all."

I mentally crossed my fingers for the fib. Garrett Simms was supercreepy. Hard to explain, but he looked like a big, hairy baby . . . but he was such a nice man. It wasn't his fault he looked like he looked.

"I know what you're thinking, Tally Jones. You're thinking that I'm close-minded and judgmental."

*Bingo.*

"But I'm telling you, Tucker Gentry chaperoned an interfaith youth group trip to South Padre Island last spring break, and my Dani got some very bad vibes from him. She was deeply shaken. To prey on her in her condition . . ." Eloise's eyes filled, and I thought she might actually start weeping.

"Oh dear," I soothed, reaching across the counter to lay a comforting hand on her arm. "I'm so sorry. I just heard about Dani. You must be beside yourself. But honestly, Eloise, you have to be careful what you say about Tucker. You could seriously damage his life with accusations like that."

She sniffed, and pulled away. "Maybe that's what he deserves."

She turned and stormed away, my pleas to her to stop so we could make amends falling on deaf ears.

I quickly fell back to scooping with Kyle, but when Beth arrived to spell us for dinner, Kyle tugged on my sleeve.

"That lady's full of crap," he said.

"What lady? And don't say 'crap.' "

We shared a smile at the absurdity of me telling him to watch his language. "Sorry, Miz Tally," he mocked gently. "That lady who was talking about Mr. Gentry."

"Eloise?"

"Yeah. Mr. Gentry is a nice guy. And he's got a girlfriend who's doing mission work in Peru. She's older than him, too." He said this last as though it were beyond comprehension, that a man might date an older woman. I decided to let it slide.

"How do you know so much about Tucker Gentry? You don't go to One Word, do you?" I was pretty sure if Kyle Mason stepped foot inside the One Word Bible Church, they'd launch a flash exorcism.

"No, but my buddy Matt's in Mr. Gentry's youth group. He talks about Mr. Gentry and his girlfriend all the time. I think Matt's going to go on some mission trip with them at Christmas. If he can convince his new secret girlfriend to go with him."

Despite myself, I was intrigued. "Secret girlfriend?"

Kyle snorted. "Matt's kind of a dork. He's real romantic."

I'd seen the way Kyle looked at Alice. If being romantic was dorky, Kyle's cool cred was gone.

"I confess, Kyle, I'm surprised you hang out with someone in an evangelical youth group."

Kyle grimaced. "Matt's okay. He's straight-edge."

"Straight-edge?"

"He's in a rock band, really hard-core, but not into

drugs and stuff. Like 'punk rock for Jesus.' He's got all these tats and piercings, but he won't drink caffeine."

"And that's okay with the One Word folks?"

"I don't know about the rest of them, but it's okay with Mr. Gentry. He even gave Matt's band a place to practice."

"I guess that is pretty cool."

"He understands the kids. Cuts 'em slack when they mess up. On that spring break trip? Those Methodist kids all got loaded at some bar called Juan McCool's. Tequila slammers. That Dani girl threw up all over the inside of the van they rented. Mr. Gentry lost the deposit."

"Dani Carberry got drunk on tequila? She's not even eighteen!"

Kyle looked at me as if I were the biggest nerd in the world. Which, I suppose, I was. Just because kids couldn't get booze legally didn't mean they couldn't get booze. Especially cute girls on spring break.

"Well, didn't she get arrested?"

"No. Like I said, Mr. Gentry's a cool guy. Not cool like I'd want to hang out with him, but okay. He didn't turn in the kids to the cops because he knew that it would make it harder for them to apply for scholarships and stuff."

I wasn't sure Tucker showed the best judgment in letting the kids off so easy, but it made me wonder why Dani Carberry and her mother would be so dead set against a man who had actually done Dani a big favor.

# chapter 11

A few hours later, Kyle and Beth were taking care of business at the fair while Grandma Peachy and her girls—me, Bree, and Alice—spent some quality time at the A-la-mode. Peachy had decided the ladies' room needed repainting, so she and Alice were in ratty shorts and T-shirts, do-rags tied around their heads, and paintbrushes in their hands.

Peachy's scrawny legs, the skin tissue-paper thin and traced with dark veins, sticking out from the hems of her saggy cargo shorts, made me want to hug her tight. It reminded me how very old she was, something I tended to forget because her mind (and her temper) was still so sharp.

"You missed a spot, little girl," she snapped, stabbing her paintbrush at a spot above Alice's head where the original white still shone through the robin's-egg blue Peachy had chosen.

"Cut me some slack, old woman," Alice quipped back. "I'm shorter than you."

Peachy cackled in delight. Peachy'd raised us to be feisty, and it pleased her that Alice had a little vinegar in her.

The bell at the door rang, and I hushed Peachy and Alice. Their good-natured sniping was fine for family, but I didn't want them scaring off customers.

But it wasn't a customer coming to visit. It was Cal McCormack. And by the grim set to his mouth, he wasn't popping in for a milk shake.

I approached him cautiously. "Hey, Cal. What's up?"

"Is Bree here?" he asked softly.

"In the back."

He glanced over my shoulder to the propped-open door of the ladies' room. Inside, Peachy and Alice were flicking paint at each other. I was going to have to pay Kyle overtime to clean up the mess they were making.

Cal cleared his throat. "Let's mosey back there and have a chat with her."

I shot Cal a questioning look, but he wouldn't meet my eyes. That was bad news, indeed.

We found Bree in the back, whistling softly as she poured a batch of cinnamon-scented custard base into a whirling vertical batch freezer. She set the empty plastic tub on the floor and, with a practiced move, lowered the long, screwlike blade into the freezer.

She grabbed the tub and turned to toss it in the industrial-sized sink, but she froze when she saw us.

Some silent exchange passed between Cal and Bree. Even knowing my cousin as well as I did, I couldn't read all the emotions that flitted across her face. But in the end, she sighed.

"Really?" she asked.

"'Fraid so," Cal replied. "I'm not gonna use the cuffs, and we can go out the back so Alice doesn't see, but . . ." He shook his head. "Listen, I don't want to do this, but better me than someone else."

"It's okay, Cal," Bree said with a sad smile. "If I'm gonna be arrested, it may as well be by a tall, handsome lawman. Like in a romance novel."

At her backhanded compliment, Cal's neck colored above his buttoned collar. "Look, this isn't a question, Bree, and I don't want you to say a word without a lawyer, but I want you to know. We pulled your phone records from the night before Kristen was murdered, looking for that call you said you got. According to the phone company, only one number called your home line. And that's a cell phone listed in the name of Alice Anders."

"What? My daughter didn't—" Bree began, but Cal cut her off with a sharply raised hand.

"Not a word. You hear. That was just information." He shot me a meaningful look.

Holy guacamole, but I thought Cal McCormack, who'd spent much of the last year trying to convince me to mind my own beeswax, was encouraging me to meddle.

"I gotta do the official stuff now." He cleared his throat again. "Bree Michaels, you are under arrest for the murder of Kristen Ver Steeg. You have the right to remain silent. Anything you say . . ."

I listened to Cal reciting the words I'd heard on the TV so many times before, my whole body numb as I watched Bree nod calmly to indicate she understood.

"Do you understand these—"

"Mama, Gram just wrote a dirty word—"

Alice tumbled into the back room just as Cal was finishing reading Bree her rights and as he was taking her gently by the arm to lead her away.

"What's going on?" Alice demanded.

"It's okay, honey. Aunt Tally will explain everything."

Dear heavens, I'd rather explain anything in the world to the girl—sex, quantum physics, politics—than why Cal was taking her mother to jail.

"Mom!" The note of panic in Alice's voice made her sound even younger than her seventeen years. Made her sound like a child. A child who needed her mommy.

"Hush, Alice," Bree soothed, even as Cal held open the back door for her. "I'll be home soon."

As the door whooshed shut behind her, I rushed to Alice and wrapped my arms around her to support her.

"It's okay, Alice," I said, praying I was telling the truth. "It's just a mistake. We'll get it straightened out soon."

Cal must have pulled some serious strings, but he managed to get Bree booked and arraigned within a few hours. Bail was set at a staggering figure we couldn't possibly afford to cover, but Finn—whose mother had transferred the deed to her house to him before moving into the nursing home—put up his suburban house as collateral on her bond.

"We're family," he explained simply. "That's what we do."

As a result, Bree was back in the bosom of her family by dinnertime.

For the first time since we'd opened, I actually shut down the A-la-mode without notice. Just posted a sheet of paper on the door that read COME VISIT US AT THE FAIR, where Beth and Kyle were holding down the fort.

The family, Finn included, gathered at the house, a pan of hastily prepared spinach lasagna, garlic bread, beer, and a plate of Peachy's butterscotch bars providing sustenance.

"What I don't understand," Bree said around a mouthful of garlic bread, "is why Kristen's call isn't showing up on the phone company's records. I swear she called me."

"Did you get any other calls that night?" Finn asked.

"That's just it. Cal said that I did get a call—from Alice. But Alice didn't call. Did you, baby?"

Alice stopped chewing midbite. She grabbed for her glass of water and washed down the lasagna that had apparently gotten stuck in her craw.

"Oh, Mama," she said. "I'm so sorry."

"What for?" Bree looked as lost as I felt.

"I lost my phone."

"So? It's just a cheapie. We'll get you a new one."

"No, I mean I lost my phone that night. The night Dad—Sonny came back to town."

"Help me out here," Bree said, a note of impatience creeping into her voice.

Pieces of the puzzle started to fall into place, and I jumped in. "After the big confrontation between you and Sonny at the fairgrounds, after you told Alice her daddy was back in town, Alice borrowed Kyle's Bonnie and took a little spin. Right?"

Alice nodded, miserable. "Yeah." She reached a hand out toward her mother, letting it rest on the dining table between them. "I know I told you I didn't care he was back, that I didn't want to see him, but I did. I didn't want to talk to him, exactly, just see him. You know?"

Bree closed the gap and settled her hand on top of Alice's. "I know, baby."

Poor Alice cleared her throat. "I drove around looking for him. I heard he was driving a nice car, a shiny red Lexus. I finally spotted it at nearly ten that night, parked at the Dutch Oven."

"Sonny always loved their pancakes," Bree muttered.

The Dutch Oven had once been a national chain pancake house, but the franchisee had gotten tired of paying money to some big corporation. He'd changed the name, painted the restaurant's A-frame roof from blue to red, and planted a windmill he'd bought from a defunct mini-golf outlet in the parking lot. I don't know how much he changed the chain's recipe, but he'd managed to avoid a lawsuit.

"I parked the Bonnie right next to the Lexus, figuring I'd wait for him. But it was hot, so I got out and sat on the hood. I saw him inside, sitting with these two ladies—one blond, one redheaded. I pulled out my phone because I'd scanned that picture of him from my baby book—the one where he's holding me and smiling?—and I had it saved on the phone. I recognized him from that picture."

Lord. No little girl should have to recognize her daddy that way, by seeing the resemblance between him and a grainy Polaroid picture.

"I was sitting there waiting, trying to figure out what I'd say, when the blond lady came out. She asked me who I was." Alice looked down in her lap, ashamed. "I said some ugly things. I don't even remember what. But I told her that the man she was having coffee with had abandoned his wife and child. That he was a horrible human being and she must be horrible, too, if she was hanging around with him.

"I slid off the hood of the Bonnie. I'm not sure whether I was going to leave, or whether I was going to storm into the Dutch Oven and pick a fight with him. But the blond lady grabbed me by the arm."

Alice swallowed hard. She kept calling the woman "the blond lady," but we all knew it was Kristen Ver Steeg she'd met in the parking lot. I wondered briefly whether depersonalizing her helped Alice cope a little.

"The lady told me that I was right. Sonny wasn't a

good guy. But she knew about bad guys, and she'd take care of it. I pulled away from her, climbed in the Bonnie, and took off.

"I pulled into the Mickey-D's parking lot just down the highway, planning to call Kyle, but my phone was gone. I must have dropped it in the parking lot."

Bree nodded. "And Kristen picked it up. That's how she got the number for the landline in my bedroom. And that's why the phone records only show one call that night, from your phone."

"I'm sorry, Mama! I should have told you I saw her that night. I should have told you I lost my phone. But I didn't know you'd get arrested because I screwed up."

Bree slid off her chair and knelt at Alice's side, pulling her daughter into a brutal hug. "Honey, you didn't screw up. And you didn't get me arrested. Cal made it clear the prosecutor got the indictment based on the physical evidence at the fair. They didn't even have the phone records when they went to the grand jury."

Finn, Peachy, and I had been silent observers during Alice's bleak confession, but Peachy finally chimed in.

"That Sonny Anders is up to no damn good. I wish I knew what dirty piece of business brought him slithering back to Dalliance and into our lives."

Finn piped up. "Funny you should mention it. Mike Carberry told me that Sonny had invited a select group of Dalliance businessmen to the Parlay Inn tonight. Said he wanted to present them with a proposition."

"A deal with the devil?" Peachy asked.

Finn grabbed my hand and gave it a squeeze. "What do you say, kiddo? Want to go see what Sonny Anders has to offer the good people of Dalliance?"

Yes. Yes, I did.

# chapter 12

The Parlay Inn buzzed with excitement. Whatever happened as the evening unfolded, it was sure to be the stuff of Dalliance legend. Sonny had thrown around enough cash and dropped enough hints that folks were mighty interested in hearing what he had to say. But those same folks also remembered him from his rockabilly, grease-monkey, petty criminal days. Those memories did not inspire confidence. Whichever way the dice fell, though, Sonny Anders was sure to spin a good story. There were a lot of white heads tipped back in expectation, a lot of beefy arms folded across barrel chests.

I didn't bar-hop much, and when I did go out for a cocktail, I tended to patronize the Bar None—with its plank floors, neon beer signs, and Wednesday karaoke. The Parlay Inn catered to a different clientele, mostly male, mostly over fifty, and mostly pretty set in their ways. Black-and-white photos of Dalliance's development, a polished brass bar rail, and an amber-tinted Wurlitzer reinforced the air of tradition.

Finn and I snagged a tiny table near the jukebox. I wanted to be out of the way, but we both wanted to hear all the details. We figured no one would be dropping quarters in the juke during Sonny's spiel.

He took the floor at five past the hour, his hands raised like those of a revival preacher blessing his flock.

"Friends," he shouted, "friends." The chatter in the bar died down, and Sonny lowered his voice a bit. But he still projected like a seasoned orator.

"Thank you all for coming out tonight. It's good to see some familiar faces here, folks I haven't seen in a good long while." His lips slid across his teeth in a Cheshire grin. "We're all a little less fired up than we used to be, but we're not quite out of gas yet. Am I right?"

A wave of backslapping and manly chuckles rippled through the room.

"Friends," he said again, "y'all know I'm just a good ol' boy with more spit than sense. But I've been blessed in my life to find a woman with a good head on her shoulders. This here's Charlize Guidry."

Char moved to stand by Sonny's side. She was dressed in a delicate dove gray suit. Teal silk peeped from the deep neck of the jacket, and the ladylike peplum hinted at delicious curves beneath the staid wool. The skirt was carefully fitted, but not too tight. No one could question the professionalism of her attire, but she somehow oozed sex nonetheless.

"Char's daddy, Remy Guidry—well, y'all may have heard tell of Remy." Sonny's chin dropped and he fixed his crowd with a knowing stare. Sure enough, a murmur of assent rose from the group, and I saw a number of heads nodding gently.

I shot Finn a look. He leaned in. "Oldest con in the book. Make people feel like they're stupid if they don't know what you're talking about, and then they're too scared of looking foolish to question you."

"Char, here, learned a thing or two at her daddy's knee. I'll let her explain."

Char stepped forward and raised her head. I don't know how she managed it, but at that precise moment, a single lock of cinnamon candy hair slipped from the tidy French twist and caressed her jaw.

No one made a peep.

"Gentlemen, there is a fortune beneath your feet. A fortune in petroleum, the food of this nation's economy. It's right there, so close you can practically taste it." The tip of her tongue darted out to lick the corner of her lip, and the whole room gasped softly. She owned them.

"The trick, as you all know, is to get that oil out of the ground. I'm sure you've all heard horror stories about fracking."

There wasn't a soul in Texas who wasn't familiar with fracking: hydraulic fracturing. Drillers pumped fluid into petroleum-rich rock at a high rate of pressure. The fluid fractured the rock, releasing the petroleum, and increasing the production of the well.

The problem was the chemicals in the fracturing fluid could contaminate the water table, could seep back to the surface and contaminate the soil and air. Not to mention concerns that breaking up rock could cause geologic events like earthquakes.

Texans aren't usually on the side of the tree huggers, but the folks in Dalliance and in lots of similar communities were leery enough of fracking that they resisted offers from oil companies to milk the shale for oil and gas . . . and money. It was one thing to muck around beneath foreign soil or the unpopulated desert to the west, but another thing entirely to pulverize the very ground beneath our feet.

Char raised a pale hand to forestall any grumbling. "I've got an alternative. One hundred percent safe."

A few murmurs of disbelief began welling up from the crowd, but Char tossed her head, sending that lock of hair bouncing, and—like magic—the room grew silent again.

"I can't say too much, because we've got six patents pending on this process, but instead of pushing the oil from the rock, it pulls the oil from the rock. We use the petroleum's own molecular structure to our advantage. The rock itself remains perfectly intact. And we replace the petroleum with a compound with the exact same molecular weight and viscosity, so the rock remains stable."

Dave Epler, chairman of Dalliance's Chamber of

Commerce and owner of half the new and used auto dealerships in town, rose to his feet, his joints creaking and grinding audibly beneath the weight of sixty years of whiskey and chicken-fried everything. He cleared his throat with a liquid "horp."

"What about that compound? What's in it?"

Char smiled and batted her lashes. "Now, sir, I sure wish I could tell you that." Her voice oozed like warm butter through the room. "But this is some pretty valuable intellectual property. What I can tell you is that I've tasted the stuff myself."

"Tasted?"

"Yessir. Tasted. Just a little lick, mind you. I wouldn't brush it on a brisket, but it didn't make me sick."

The whole crowd rustled and muttered, the swell of noise reaching a crescendo before subsiding in the face of Sonny's raised hands.

"I told you, folks, she's a smart cookie," he quipped.

Dave shifted from one trunklike leg to the other and raised a hand of his own. "Let's cut the bull crap," he barked, chopping the air to punctuate his command. "What's on the table? Why are you here?"

Sonny cupped his hand around Char's elbow and guided her back to her seat, the noble gentleman and his lady. "All righty," he said when she had settled in, "let's get down to brass tacks.

"I met Ms. Guidry up in Pennsylvania where she was making a tidy fortune for a small private gas production firm. I was providing some related services for those gentlemen, and I realized what a gem they had on their hands. But they were small-minded men with no real vision. They knew the natural gas fields of the Midwest, but were too timid to tackle the real honeypot down here in the Altemont Shale."

Sonny propped a foot on the seat of a chair, and braced his hand on his knee. "Char and I have bigger plans, and that's why we're here."

Dave grumbled. "So you want us to sign over our leases? Let you drill on our land?"

Sonny wagged his head back and forth. "No, sir. Me and Char, we want to bring the good people of Dalliance in as equal partners."

Now Mike Carberry stood, angling his way to Dave Epler's side. "Why? If this is such a surefire thing, why make us partners?"

Sonny brushed some imaginary lint from the knee of his pants. "Look," he said, "I could feed you some line of bullshit about it being the right thing to do and wanting to give back to the community and all that nonsense. But y'all weren't born yesterday."

That drew a few appreciative chuckles from the audience.

"Truth is, Charlize and I have some contractual encumbrances. See, we worked with that outfit up in PA, and we had noncompete clauses in our contracts. I consulted with counsel both up north and here. Ms. Kristen Ver Steeg."

He paused while a few folks crossed themselves, ducked their heads, or swiped off their hats at the invocation of the dead.

"The lawyers talked a lot of Latin to us, but at the end of the day it boiled down to something pretty simple. They explained that we cannot utilize Ms. Guidry's technology for profit in our own names. But there's a little loophole in that contract. See, as long as Charlize and I are not the majority shareholders of any competing enterprise, that clause doesn't kick in. So we've set up a corporation, y'all buy shares in the corporation—invest capital in exchange for a share of the profits—then we license the technology to the corporation, which is totally legit, and God willing—we all get rich."

"What's the catch?" Dave said, and the crowd behind him murmured its support. "You're not talking to a bunch of wet-behind-the-ears venture capitalists. We've all been around the block a time or two, and we know there's no such thing as a perfect deal."

Sonny nodded gravely. "You're right, Dave. And I respect you too much to sugarcoat this. This here's a time-sensitive deal. Those fellas up in Pennsylvania, they weren't too eager to expand their business into Texas. Some sort of tax issue. But they have investors, too, who might want to go it alone. Or the Pennsylvania guys might decide the profit is worth the risk. We gotta strike now, while the iron's hot.

"And"—he held up his hands—"Char and I, we've put a lot of our sweat and heart into this deal. The tech's all hers, and I put up the money for the lawyers for the patents and to do the land work down here. We don't want to carve up this pie too much. So we're only taking six partners, at ten percent each, for a total of sixty percent of the deal. The other forty percent, that's me and Char. We're limiting people to a single ten percent buy-in, and no married couples or blood relatives. We don't want our partners ganging up and forcing us out of this deal."

"Numbers," Dave barked.

"Twenty grand gets you in."

Someone from the back of the room shouted out, "What happened to the 'good people of Dalliance'?"

Sonny's lips twisted in a wry smile. "Like I said, friends, we're not saints. We're entrepreneurs. I'm happy some of my old buddies get to enjoy some profit here, but this is our project. Our bottom line."

Charlize stood and smoothed her hands over her skirt, her hair. Sonny started moving through the crowd, handing out business cards. Finn waved at Mike Carberry, indicating Mike should snag one of those cards for him. "We're staying out at the Ramada," Sonny announced, raising his voice to be heard over the hubbub of folks gathering their things. "Time is of the essence."

I laid a hand on Finn's forearm. "No one's gonna buy that load of crap, are they?"

Finn shook his head. "You'd be surprised what people will fall for."

"But surely with the Internet and all, it wouldn't take two seconds to poke holes in their story."

He shrugged. "I bet not. What did they really tell us? Her daddy's Remy Guidry. South Louisiana is crawling with Guidrys, half of them named Remy . . . surely one or two of them made a little cash in the oil boom of the late seventies. And they're using fracking all over the Midwest, but those companies don't disclose the formulas for the fluids they use. It's proprietary stuff.

Very hush-hush. No way to prove or disprove that Charlize Guidry created a miracle technique for extracting gas from shale. At least, not in a few days."

My purchase of the A-la-mode aside, I was pretty careful with my money. I'd always been the voice of reason, stopping my highly inebriated mama from investing in some pyramid scheme or spending her whole savings on lottery scratch-offs, giving Alice savings bonds and certificates of deposit for every birthday, and planning my week to take advantage of double coupon day at Albertsons. I couldn't fathom that anyone would invest twenty thousand dollars on Sonny Anders's flimflam show.

"What's that old saying, if it's too good to be true, then it probably is?"

Finn wrapped his arm around my shoulders and pulled me close. "But all these guys, especially the old-timers, they all know a guy, maybe a friend of a friend, who got rich off of oil. Working guy, not too bright, not doing anything special, and then one day he wakes up a millionaire. You hear those stories, you have to believe it can happen to you. Someone comes to you with a get-rich-quick scheme, and it seems completely feasible."

Finn was right. At least a couple of hopeful souls in the bar that night would raid their retirement funds with the hopes of striking it rich. And by setting a limit to the number of investors, Sonny made it seem as if he wasn't being greedy while at the same time guaranteeing that folks felt pressured to act fast.

I could see the scam as clear as day, but people fell for scams all the time. How many fake Nigerian princes had fleeced well-meaning, generally intelligent people out of their life savings? By comparison, Sonny and Char's story sounded pretty plausible.

# *chapter 13*

The next day, as they say, the show had to go on. With the prospect of serious legal fees looming, we couldn't keep the A-la-mode closed, and we needed to man the booth at the fair, so we had all hands on deck. In addition, my judge duties were finally kicking into high gear, so I had to make a midday run to the Creative Arts pole barn to do the official tasting for the hand-cranked ice cream and stone fruit preserve categories.

The powers that be had persuaded Jackie Conway, whose husband owned Conway Chrysler-Pontiac-Jeep, to fill Kristen's shoes. Jackie was good friends with Garrett Simms's wife, JoAnne, and I guessed there had been some pressure brought to bear on Jackie, because I couldn't imagine she was particularly pleased to be spending her day in the pole barn—which, truth be told, smelled ever so faintly of manure.

Jackie greeted me with a dazzling smile, as bright and fake as a silver Christmas tree. I happened to know the woman thought I was one step from white trash and capable of murder. Still, I did my best to smile back.

"Isn't this so exciting?" Jackie gushed.

I looked at the people milling around the judges' table: Garrett Simms with his perpetual hangdog expression, a harried woman with a clipboard and a pencil holding her hair in a bun, Tucker and Eloise shooting daggers at each other, a bored college-age kid with an Ed Hardy T-shirt and a press pass (undoubtedly an unpaid intern from the *News-Letter*).

"Positively thrilling, Jackie," I deadpanned.

Her face froze in its fake smile for a second, and I could practically see the gears turning behind her eyes, before she doubled over in genuine laughter.

She grabbed my arm and pulled me close. "Lord a'mighty," she whispered, "I'm so glad I'm not the only one who'd rather be elsewhere. When Kristen asked me to take over for her, I had no idea what I was getting myself into."

Despite the smothering heat, I felt a chill slither down my spine. "Kristen?" I gasped.

Jackie tipped her head in puzzlement.

"I, uh, I just assumed someone had asked you to fill in after Kristen died," I explained.

"Oh dear, no. Kristen didn't ask me from the grave. She called me on the telephone the day before she died. Asked me to fill in for her on this judging panel and with the Rodeo Pageant. Not sure who gave her my name. Probably JoAnne Simms, getting payback for me roping her into that wretched charity auction for the greyhound rescue."

She shivered dramatically. "If I'd given it any thought, I would have said no. This is torture, plain and simple. Garrett's always so serious about everything, you know. And that one"—she jerked her head subtly in the direction of the woman with the clipboard—"she's been buzzing around here muttering about rocks and hard places."

"What's wrong with her?" I asked.

"Not sure. But I think both Tucker and Eloise have been taking out their hatred of each other on her. Invoking rules and regulations in a petty bureaucratic war. That poor girl is just the cannon fodder."

"What's the deal between those two?"

"Eloise and Tucker? I don't know," Jackie said. "But they're gunning for each other."

"I know Eloise has it in for Tucker, but does the animosity run both ways?"

"Oh my, yes," Jackie said, her eyes alight with glee. "As chair of the League of Methodist Ladies, Eloise is on the all-faith youth group coordinating committee with Tucker. I hear she's even more tyrannical there than she usually is, because Dani is a youth group leader."

Jackie's head swiveled and I followed her line of sight. A teenage girl lurked at the edge of the crowd. Dani Carberry.

Dani resembled her mother just enough to eliminate any doubt of kinship. But in Dani, Eloise's strong features were softened a bit, and the formfitting T-shirt and jeans she wore showed just a hint of curve to her slim figure. With a fall of thick mahogany hair, she looked like a Hollywood vision of Pocahontas: striking, athletic, strong.

The hair, though, I had to remind myself, was a wig. A really good wig. And she didn't appear sick otherwise. She was thin, but thin the way teenage girls want to be, not bony. She was hiding her illness well.

"That Dani didn't fall far from the maternal tree. She's just as bossy and entitled as her mother. Though it is too bad about the cancer."

Jackie *tsk*ed softly.

"Well, like I was saying, Tucker has it in for Eloise. She volunteered to chaperone a youth group camping trip to the Dinosaur Park this summer." About an hour outside Fort Worth, there's a big state park where you can see fossilized brontosaurus footprints. It's a popular destination for youth campers. "Tucker vetoed it."

"I don't think the One Word Bible Church is down with the dinosaurs," I suggested.

Jackie gave me a playful nudge. "True enough. Their contingent was planning a side trip to the creationist museum right by the park. Tucker didn't veto the trip. He vetoed Eloise chaperoning."

"Really? Why?"

"Apparently he wouldn't say. But he was adamant, if Eloise was in charge, the One Word youth group wouldn't participate. And since One Word's group is the biggest, them pulling out would make it tough for the rest of the groups to cover the overhead—the bus, the campsite fees, and the like. Eloise backed down."

"Ouch."

"Yeah, major blow to her ego. Not to mention that it got all the churchy crowd tittering about what terrible sin Eloise might have committed to make Tucker react the way he did."

"No one has any idea at all?"

"None. It's a genuine mystery."

"Huh."

"Ladies," Garrett called from across the room. "It's time for us to get started. Grab your spoons, and let's roll."

I glanced over at Tucker and Eloise, facing each other like generals on the battlefield. I knew that there was a lot more at stake in that ice cream competition than a blue ribbon and bragging rights.

Jackie, Garrett, and I sat side by side at a table at one end of the pole barn. The table squatted atop a low platform, so we had a good view of the crowd sitting in ranks of folding chairs in front of us. Given the setup and the grim faces staring back at us, I felt as if we were the parole board facing a roomful of unlikely felons. Except our table was draped with star-spangled bunting, and instead of criminal case files, the harried clipboard-toting woman was bringing us little paper dishes of ice cream.

Each dish contained a single scoop of ice cream. We ate with small plastic spoons, a fresh one for each dish.

And we were encouraged to cleanse our palates between entries by munching on small unsalted pretzel twists and sipping tepid water.

For each entry, we filled out a detailed scorecard, rating the scoops on a scale of one to ten for texture (the mouth feel of the ice cream), taste (the quality of the ingredients), and flavor (the originality and harmony of the component ingredients). We made detailed notes about iciness, gumminess, excessive carmelization of the lactose from overcooking, balance of salty and sweet.

The whole enterprise seemed very scientific. Though, of course, it came down to our personal preferences . . . and there was nothing scientific about that.

The audience seemed to hold its collective breath when the aide placed dishes of Tucker's Pepper Praline ice cream before us.

I looked at the scoop first. It was a pretty ice cream, a lovely rich ivory color with clearly defined ribbons of a pale brown-sugar caramel and tiny flecks of rust-colored ground pepper.

But I knew as soon as I dipped my spoon into the scoop that Tucker was in trouble. The spoon stuttered as it moved through the ice cream. The texture lacked the silky glide of good ice cream, crumbling a bit as it rested in the bowl of my spoon. Sure enough, as I held the taste in my mouth, it felt too cold with the sandy feel of ice crystals.

And then the pepper hit me.

Maybe it was just the bite I got, but the heat overwhelmed me, scorching every taste bud in my mouth.

I gasped and reached for the water, knocking over the cup in my haste.

As I snatched up the cup and fumbled with the pitcher to pour myself some more, I looked around in panic. My eyes found Eloise Carberry sitting in the very front row.

It might be irrational, but the look of smug glee on her face ticked me off. If I'd stopped to think about it, I would have realized she was rejoicing in Tucker's failure. But that jolt of cayenne had well and truly stripped my good sense away, and in that instant, it felt as if Eloise was laughing at my discomfort.

Which was mean.

"You okay?" Garrett asked softly.

"Yes," I gasped.

He reached out to steady my hand and took the pitcher from me, pouring me more water.

"Definitely not your recipe," he deadpanned.

I glanced up and found Garrett's eyes, the pale opaque blue of old milk glass, watching me with quiet amusement. I'd never thought of Garrett as having a sense of humor, but I guess when you look like an overgrown Howdy Doody doll, you have to adopt a certain wry attitude.

"No," I choked. "Definitely not mine."

Eloise's peach-pecan ice cream came next. After Tucker's brutal assault on my taste buds, I hoped Eloise's sweet confection would hit the spot. But she'd over-reduced the peaches with way too much brown sugar. The syrupy fruit overwhelmed all the other flavors in the dish. It wasn't terrible, but it didn't exactly light my fire.

It turned out the hand-cranked ice cream competition did not vindicate either Tucker or Eloise. Instead, much to everyone's surprise, a thirteen-year-old girl swept the entire category, winning first prize for a piña colada ice cream I would have been proud to serve at the A-la-mode. She also won second place for her Mexican chocolate ice cream and third for an old-fashioned butter pecan.

Mentally, I made a note that I would either need to hire the child or face some serious competition in my future.

As Garrett read the results, I kept my eye on Tucker and Eloise. Not surprisingly, the two were splitting their own attention between Garrett and each other.

I just couldn't imagine what had prompted this feud of theirs. I knew better than to think it had to be something big. After all, even the smallest slight or perceived injustice could work its way under your skin like a sliver and fester there. My mama and my aunt Jenny quarreled bitterly right up until the day my mama drank herself to death, and neither one of them could—or would—tell anyone what had soured their relationship.

As Garrett awkwardly hung the winners' medallions over thirteen-year-old Emma Christy's pigtailed head, Eloise stood up from her chair too fast, causing the steel legs to clatter against the concrete floor. She reached down to her daughter, who sat at her side, and grabbed Dani by the wrist.

When her mother yanked her to her feet, Dani reached up a hand to steady her wig on her head in the same way a person might clasp a hat on tight in the face of a strong wind.

I couldn't hear their exchange, but mother and daughter seemed to be sharing some sharp words.

After a moment of back-and-forth, Eloise stalked across the front of the audience, heading toward the door at the far side of the room.

Tucker Gentry, still sitting quietly with hands folded as though in prayer, sat at the far end of the front row. Eloise and Dani had to walk past him to get out.

As they did, Tucker raised his chin. He faced forward, head never moving, but I could see his eyes tracking their progress. Eloise didn't condescend to spare him a glance.

But Dani did.

She raised her free hand, the one not clasped in her mother's fierce grip, and waggled her fingers in Tucker's direction. A wave. Small, but unmistakable.

Then she took a running step to catch up with the brisk pace set by her mother, and the two of them disappeared from sight.

"Weird, huh?"

I jumped at Jackie Conway's voice at my elbow.

"I'll say," I replied.

"Lot of weird stuff in Dalliance these days."

Sonny Anders waltzing back to town.

A zombie cowboy killing a gorgeous young lawyer.

Finn Harper telling me he loved me.

Weird stuff, indeed.

# *chapter 14*

As I schlepped my way to the fair parking lot after the competition, a posh mica gray Audi slid up beside me. The tinted window on the passenger side glided down with a soft *whoosh* and a wave of arctic air wafted out.

"Hey, hot stuff, can I give you a lift?"

My friend Deena Silver peered at me over the rims of her bright purple sunglasses. One plump, persimmon-manicured hand rested lightly on the Audi's leather steering wheel, a tangle of copper bangle bracelets swaying gently in the gale-force blast of the car's air-conditioning. As usual, Deena was garbed in flowing, gauzy robes, veils of periwinkle and aqua draping her earth-mother roundness.

Deena and I were fellow travelers. We'd met when we'd worked together to cater my ex-husband's company picnic. I did dessert, and Deena's popular catering company provided the rest of the food and drink. Deena and I discovered that our kinship transcended a love of tasty food. We'd quickly become genuine friends.

"Where you heading?" I asked.

"Just over to Jackson and Ver Steeg with a Bundt cake. Jason's been clerking with them while he waits for the results of his bar exam." Deena's daughter had just married Jason, a recent law school grad, earlier in the summer. "Under the circumstances, I thought you might want to tag along."

"The circumstances?"

"Oh, don't play coy with me, young lady. I know your penchant for snooping, and I've heard a thing or two about how Ms. Ver Steeg died."

I'd been relieved that Jackie didn't mention Bree's arrest, but I knew it was just a matter of time before the whole town heard. I phrased my question carefully. "Anything particular?"

Deena sighed. "I play canasta with Vonda Hudson from the 911 call center. I got the skinny about Bree last night. I'd say the news will go viral by late this afternoon." She patted the black leather passenger seat. "Come on. I'd bet good money you'd appreciate an excuse to visit Kristen's office. Besides, a slice of my lemon Bundt is worth a little detour on your way home."

With a grateful smile, I pulled open the passenger door and slid into the blissful cool of the car's front seat. As I tugged the door closed, Deena used one acrylic nail to raise the window, sealing us inside.

"I didn't know Jason was working with Madeline and Kristen," I said.

Deena slid her glasses back up her nose and edged forward through the dusty parking lot.

"Well, he's cheap labor right now. Poor kid graduated with a law degree when law jobs are thin on the ground, and until he gets that letter from the State Bar saying he passed, he really can't do much of anything. They've been paying him minimum wage to do legal research and draft motions."

"Minimum wage? Heck, I pay Kyle better than that."

Deena chuckled. "Scut-work for Jackson and Ver Steeg will look better on Jason's résumé than scooping ice cream for you. And he's been making a little extra cash bartending for me." Deena ran a popular catering company, the Silver Spoon. "Thankfully, Crystal's mama loves her a lot and won't let her and her new groom go hungry."

"Does Jason like what he's doing?"

She laughed louder. "Cut the crap. You don't care a bit about Jason's job satisfaction. You want the skinny on Kristen Ver Steeg."

"Busted," I admitted with a smile.

Deena shrugged. "Jason says Kristen and Madeline are struggling a bit. New legal practice and all. And after the scandal with Madeline's uncle, they lost some clients."

Ridiculous as it was, I felt a pang of guilt. Madeline Jackson's uncle had been bilking the local university and the federal government for serious money for a number of years. After his efforts to cover his tracks resulted in the deaths of two of Alice's friends, my snooping led to his arrest. It wasn't my fault that Madeline's uncle was a thief and a murderer, but I still felt responsible for her business woes.

"Is it bad?"

"Definitely bad. Jason's gotten a couple of postdated paychecks, and he was grumbling about the firm letting its license for the high-end online legal research service lapse. He's sneaking into the Dickerson U library to use the more barebones academic version of the service, but he feels pretty slimy doing it.

"As a result," Deena continued, "they can't be very choosy about their clients. Jason can't say much about the workload—privilege and all—but he's hinted that they're taking any and all comers."

"That's pretty normal for a law firm, though, right?"

A shrug rippled through Deena's voluptuous body. "Look, Jason's not supposed to talk about his work, but he's not exactly a crack poker player, you know? Sitting at the dinner table, he'll drop a little tidbit of interesting information, like maybe he just stumbled across it in the paper or something . . . but it's clearly related to a case. Well, the other day, Jason starts in about this fascinating nonprofit organization founded by retired Texas judges that provides advice about legal ethics questions."

"Subtle."

"I know. He's such a good boy, and smart, too, but not very canny. He didn't come right out and say it, but I think Jackson and Ver Steeg had taken on a case that was making Jason's ethics radar ping. They're young lawyers. They can't afford to play fast and loose with the rules of ethics. They don't have the kind of friends who will keep them from being disbarred."

"So they must be pretty desperate," I said.

"Yep. Pretty darned desperate."

"And now one of the partners is dead."

"Yeah," Deena said, "I wonder what Kristen's death does to the firm's bottom line."

I slipped into the Law Offices of Jackson and Ver Steeg, drafting in Deena's sweeping wake. She held a beribboned cake box in one hand and waved the other in a grand gesture worthy of a game-show hostess.

"What can I do to help?" she asked, without preamble and to no one in particular.

Jason Arbaugh, Deena's son-in-law, was wedged behind a pressboard desk in the office entry. He had a solid build, but boyish with his smooth cheeks, round-framed spectacles, and baby blond brush cut. Honest, if you'd shoved him into a Cub Scout uniform, he could have passed as a husky fifth grader. But instead of a yellow kerchief and a slew of merit badges, he wore a slightly shiny gray suit, the button tugging across his middle, and a blue-and-red-striped tie.

He pried himself out of the too-small desk chair and moved forward to unburden Deena of her cake.

"Hey, Mama," he said, bussing her on the cheek.

"Hey, boy," she replied fondly. "We've come to offer our condolences."

Jason threw a glance at the hallway leading to the

rest of the office. "Everyone's really busted up," he said, voice low. "I think Neck's gonna lose it."

"Nick the Neck is here?" I asked.

Jason nodded and rolled his eyes. "He's here all the time."

"Does he work here?"

"Technically, no. He's got his own business, Hard Case Legal Services. Does some investigation work, private security, process-serving. That's what we use him for."

"Don't you need a license to do those things? I thought Neck had a record." My recollection was that Nick DeWinter left school because he was arrested, but sometimes history gets twisted in small towns.

Jason checked the hall again. "He did," he whispered. "But it was all petty stuff, a long time ago. Kristen helped him get it expunged." He shook his head. "Guy worships her."

I remembered how protective—possessive, even—Neck had seemed when he and Kristen had served Bree with the paternity suit. They seemed like an unlikely couple, beauty and the beast, but there was truth to the old saw that "opposites attract." I wondered if Kristen returned Neck's regard with equal fervor.

"We got your flowers, Ms. Jones," Jason said. "I'm sure Maddie would want to thank you in person. Let me run and grab her."

"Oh, I hate to bother her." True, I didn't want to bother her. But I was itching to meet Madeline Jackson. I'd heard so much about her from her aunt, Rosemary Gunderson, and I was intrigued by the woman who now shouldered the weight of this law office all on her own.

"Jason, honey, rather than you bringing Maddie to us, why don't we just poke our heads in her office and say hey? We'll be in and out in a jiff, and that way we don't drag the poor woman away from her desk."

Jason glanced nervously down the hallway, clearly wondering whether giving us license to roam the office would be better or worse than going and fetching Maddie. Just then, though, the phone on the tiny reception desk rang. He sighed, reached over to pick up the handset, and waved us down the hall.

The physical offices in which Jackson and Ver Steeg operated were small but in a nice, new office complex. The walls shone with an eggshell coating of neutral cream paint, and the dark taupe carpet still gave off a faint chemical smell. Maddie and Kristen had decorated with inoffensive—and inexpensive—prints of Impressionist paintings. For a law office, it was surprisingly feminine.

Which is why Neck's hulking presence in the conference room seemed particularly jarring. The door stood wide open, revealing a room with barely enough space for the glass-topped table—the sort you purchase in pieces with a single Allen wrench and instructions in Swedish—and a handful of cheap, metal-framed chairs. A polished brass bowl filled with green glass marbles and branches of curly willow adorned the middle of the table. And Neck sprawled in one of the metal-framed chairs, his huge body draped over the table as though he'd passed out there.

We had just moved past the door, Deena in the lead,

when another voice from inside the conference room halted us both in our tracks.

"Keep it together, Nick," the unseen woman hissed. "We're on thin ice here."

"I loved her," the leather-clad side of beef at the table moaned.

The woman sighed. "Yeah, well, clearly she didn't love you back."

Neck raised his head then, the retort stirring him to life, and I found myself staring into the flat black eyes of Neck DeWinter. The harsh geometry of his face was broken by furrows of pain, and his reptilian eyes were red-rimmed.

Neck had been crying. "Who the eff are you?"

I almost piddled on that new taupe carpet. "I—uh, I'm . . ."

Deena, God love her, pushed past me in a flurry of jingling jewelry and billowing skirts. "I'm Deena Silver, and you must be the boy they call Neck. I'm Jason's mama-in-law, and I just wanted to stop by to offer my condolences. And bring you a little cake. You look like you could use a slice of cake, honey."

The flood of syrupy sympathy knocked some of the starch out of Neck, and his oil-slick eyes filled with tears.

"Oh, darlin'," Deena gushed as she bustled around the table and enveloped Neck in a motherly hug.

By that point, the other occupant of the room had stepped forward: a young woman with a halo of dark curls and a smattering of freckles across her broad, plain face. The sensible heels on her navy pumps brought her eye-to-eye with me, so she couldn't have been more than five-three in stocking feet. A navy crepe sheath dress topped with a matching open jacket revealed a sturdy body and the telltale bulge at her midsection where her control-top panty hose gave way to unconstrained tummy.

Only her brilliant blue eyes that blazed with intelligence—and a healthy dose of suspicion—saved Maddie Jackson from being as neutral and forgettable as the museum souvenir prints on the walls of her neutral, forgettable office.

"And you are . . . ?"

I forced myself to step forward and offer my hand. "I'm Tally Jones. I'm a friend of Deena's and I worked a bit with Kristen on stuff at the fair. We were both judges in the edibles competition. I, uh, wanted to offer my sympathies. I don't know if Kristen has family nearby . . ." I let my voice trail off, inviting her to volunteer information.

"No. No family."

"Oh. Well. I'm real sorry."

"So you said." Maddie Jackson wasn't even pretending to be civil. She crackled with barely suppressed annoyance.

"Can I dish you all up some cake?" Deena offered, her generous arms still wrapped around Neck's broad shoulders.

Maddie turned to face her. "I appreciate the offer, but as you can imagine, I have a lot of business matters to attend to. If you'll excuse me . . . ?"

"Of course," Deena said.

Maddie nudged her way around me, but turned back before heading toward her office. "Nick. Remember what I said."

Deena was patting Neck, cooing softly to him, and I continued to loiter nervously when the slam of Maddie's office door rattled the brass centerpiece on the conference table.

"She's real shook up," Deena said. "Bless her heart."

*Bless your heart* is the all-purpose Texanism. While it's true that sometimes a cigar is just a cigar, and "bless your heart" is sometimes a genuine benediction, it's also code for "you're dumb as a stump," "you're bass-ackward wrong," "you're pitiable and sad," and "I'm just a hairbreadth away from smackin' you upside your head." In this case, I think Deena was using it in the "smackin' upside the head" sense of the expression.

Neck took her more literally. "She's all business, that one. Not at all like Kristen."

"You and Kristen were close?" Deena asked.

His big shoulders sagged. "She was an angel," he choked.

"She sure was pretty," I said. "I heard she was a beauty queen."

"She was *my* beauty queen."

I locked eyes with Deena over the poor beast's head. Heartbreaking. No other word for it. The big man had crumbled before our eyes, destroyed by the loss of the woman he so clearly loved. And, from what Maddie had said, the love was one-sided.

Never thought I'd feel bad for a badass like Neck DeWinter, but at that moment, I surely did.

He shook himself, shaking off his funk as a retriever shakes off lake water. With a liquid sniff he stood, sending Deena back a step to accommodate his truly staggering size.

"I gotta work," he said curtly. He reached into his inside jacket pocket for his sunglasses, which neatly hid the telltale signs of grief. As he pulled out the glasses, though, a white scrap of paper followed and fluttered to the carpeting.

Before Deena could huff and puff her way to the floor to retrieve the paper, Neck had already muscled his way around the dainty conference table and past me, heading for the front of the office.

Deena gasped for oxygen as she rose with the paper—a torn envelope, its plastic address window crackling softly as she handled it—and passed it across the table to me.

I snatched it, and hustled after Neck to give it back. But the darker angel of my snooping self forced me to glance at the scrap in my hand, to read the note written on it in pencil, the printing painfully childish:

> *Collect: E. Collins, J. Solis, Scar*
> *P. Serves: B. Michaels, T. Gentry*

"Neck," I called, before my brain had processed what my eyes had seen.

He stopped, his body filling the narrow hallway,

sealing off any hope of escape. A finger of fear tickled up my spine.

As he pivoted slowly to face me, two things happened in rapid succession. First, I realized I held Neck's "to do" list and Bree wasn't the only one he had served with court papers. Someone was suing Tucker Gentry. And second, following hot on that realization, I impulsively crumpled the envelope in my hand, hiding it from sight.

"Neck," I repeated to his face—his scary, scary face. "I'm real sorry about Kristen. She'll be missed."

He didn't flinch, didn't respond, just spun around and plowed out of the office.

I hadn't even realized I was holding my breath until it left me in a rush.

Deena sidled up next to me. "So, Velma . . . did we nab a clue?"

"Velma?"

"Jinkies," she exclaimed, holding her hand to her chest in mock surprise. "Clearly I'm Daphne."

I chuckled, relief making me a little giddy. "Grab your keys, Daphne. I think we need Fred's input."

# chapter 15

Oddly, we tracked down Finn at the A-la-mode. He'd camped out at a table in the back, laptop flipped open, sweating glass of iced tea at his side.

"No ice cream?" I chided as I leaned down to kiss the top of his head.

He patted his flat stomach. "What's that song lyric? 'She's like a baby, I'm like a cat . . . when we are happy, we both get fat.'"

"Are you saying I'm fat?"

Deena, right behind me, whistled low. "You better watch it, boy. She'll trim your nuts just like a cat, if you aren't careful."

"Yeah," I said. "I felt bad when I did it to Sherbet. But you . . . ?" Finn laughed, and I kissed his head again. "What are you doin' here?"

"Waiting for you. I want to take you on a date tonight." He snatched my hand, kissed my fingers, and then held our clasped hands to his heart. "Tally Decker Jones, will you go to the fair with me tonight?"

I ran the fingers of my free hand through the dark locks of hair that perpetually fell in his eyes. "I'll wear something pretty," I said with a smile.

"Awwww," Deena sighed. "If you two are gonna give me diabetes, I better have a big ol' sundae now, while I still can."

"I've got just the thing for you," I said. "While I'm making Deena's ice cream, take a look at this." I handed the crumpled envelope to Finn. "What do you make of it?"

Deena settled her girth onto one of my wrought-iron café chairs, and Finn smoothed out the envelope, studying it with a frown, while I slipped behind the counter of the A-la-mode to work a little ice cream magic. I dished up two scoops of straight vanilla bean ice cream—a superior vanilla made by heat-steeping the cream with vanilla bean before making the custard base—in a long, narrow banana split bowl. Then I dipped into my well of brandied cherries. Finally, I drizzled a scant ladle of bittersweet fudge sauce over the top. The result, a frozen cherry cordial. Perfect for the flamboyant Deena Silver.

I set the dish in front of her, and she dug in with gusto . . . and a moan of pure carnal passion. I sipped the iced tea I'd poured for myself and smiled. I wanted to please all my customers, but pleasing the genuine foodies was a special thrill.

"So? What do you think, Finn?" I asked.

"Should I ask where you got this?"

"I didn't steal it, if that's what you're implying. A gentleman dropped it, I retrieved it, and I haven't yet returned it."

"Mmm-hmm. I think you might be using the term 'gentleman' in a fairly loose sense. These names after the note to collect? E. Collins is surely Eddie Collins."

I had met Eddie Collins the year before. He'd given me Sherbet, actually, just a kitten at the time. He was a slightly shady guy, but generally harmless.

"And J. Solis is probably Juan Solis. Scar's a little tougher." He tapped his forehead with his index finger. "Thankfully, your man has a big brain. See, the one thing Eddie Collins and Juan Solis have in common, besides a general lack of upward mobility, is a known proclivity for dealing drugs. Eddie sticks to dealing pot, thanks to his connections back in California. Juan Solis is a wannabe gangbanger, and he peddles coke and crack here in Dalliance on behalf of the Seventy-Fives."

"The Seventy-Fives?"

"Latino gang based in Dallas. All the Dallas zip codes start with seventy-five," he explained.

"So we've got a coke dealer and a pot dealer on this list. That would suggest that maybe, just maybe, Scar is actually Daniel Skarsgaard."

"Why do I know that name?" Deena mused, a spoonful of cherry sundae halfway between the dish and her lips.

"Danny boy owns a piece of scrub property out in the county. Inherited it from an uncle. His neighbors aren't too happy about his upkeep."

"Oh, of course," Deena said. "I thought Tom was going to lynch that boy himself." Deena's husband, Tom Silver, owned a horse ranch out in the county. He was sort of the unofficial spokesman for the ranchers and gentleman farmers who rounded out the Lantana County countryside.

"What am I missing?" I said.

"Daniel Skarsgaard cooks meth. Sells it in town here, but also exports a fair bit to Dallas, Fort Worth, and even Austin," Finn explained.

"Why hasn't he been arrested?"

"Oh, everyone knows what he's doing, but he's got a veritable compound out there. Razor wire, dogs, the works. Who knows what sort of file law enforcement has on him? But they haven't made a move yet. I don't know if they're still gathering evidence or if he's got some sort of deal in the works. But, for now, he's out there with his Aryan buddies, trying not to blow himself up."

"So, three drug dealers. Why would Neck have the names of three drug dealers on his to-do list?" Deena mused.

Finn groaned. "Neck DeWinter? You two were lurking around Neck DeWinter? Hand to God, Tally, you're going to take years off my life."

Deena and I ignored Finn's melodramatic outburst.

"Doesn't Neck do work for bail bondsmen? Maybe he was supposed to pick these guys up?" I said.

"No," Finn chimed in. "I just saw Eddie at the fair yesterday. He was riding the merry-go-round and eating cotton candy. I think he was stoned. But he was definitely walking around free. And I'd have heard something down at the paper if the authorities were scooping up three drug dealers in one fell swoop. That's front-page stuff in Dalliance."

"So if he wasn't collecting the people on the list, what was he collecting?" Deena asked.

"Look, this is all real interesting," I said. "But what about the other half of the list? Neck served court papers on Bree—B. Michaels. And on Tucker Gentry. Who's suing Tucker? And for what?"

"I've got a friend in the clerk's office at the county court," Finn said. "I'll give her a call. If someone filed a lawsuit, there will be a file."

Finn flipped open his cell to make his call.

"These cherries are delicious," Deena whispered. "What do you do to them?"

"Trade secret," I replied with a smile.

Just then the little bell over the shop door tinkled. A guy in a yellow-and-orange courier uniform stepped in, a Tyvek envelope crisscrossed with preprinted green tape clutched in his hand. Sweat dripped from beneath the band of his billed cap, and the heat had turned the acne on his cheeks to a raging, painful crimson.

"Can I help you?" I said, crossing to greet him.

"I've got a package for Bree Michaels," the young courier said.

"I can sign for it." I reached to take the envelope, but he pulled it back.

"No, ma'am. This has to be signed for by the ad-
dressee. No exceptions." He sniffed and hitched up his
belt. This was as much power as a courier got to wield,
so I let him enjoy his moment.

"Well, Bree's on the schedule for this evening. She'll
be in at five thirty. Do you deliver that late?"

"Yes, ma'am. Until six."

He was talking to me, but his eyes were on my display freezer.

"Would you like a cone to go?" I asked. "On the
house."

"Really?" He frowned. "I still can't give you the package."

I struggled to keep a straight face. "I wouldn't dream
of asking you to compromise your integrity." He blushed,
his poor acne-marked cheeks turning an even angrier
shade, almost the color of ripe mulberries. "Just a scoop
of chocolate, to say thank you for braving the weather."

"Strawberry?"

I did laugh then. "Sure, strawberry."

By the time I'd dipped up the kid's strawberry cone
and sent him on his way, Finn was off the phone.

"So?" I said. "Who's suing Tucker?"

Finn frowned. "Not sure. There's a lawsuit, and Jackson and Ver Steeg is listed as the counsel of record who
filed the complaint. Specifically, Kristen Ver Steeg. But
the file itself is sealed."

"So there's no way to find out what it's about?"

"Not really. But I asked my friend why a civil suit
might be sealed, and she said the only two reasons she
knew about were if there were big-time trade secrets

involved or if the case involved a juvenile. I can't imagine a youth pastor having access to important trade secrets. But access to youth? You bet."

Holy crap. Maybe Eloise was right about Tucker having a thing for teenage girls. And maybe one of those girls' families had hired Kristen to take Tucker down.

Which meant Tucker had at least as big a motive to kill Kristen as Bree did.

## *chapter 16*

The Ferris wheel climbed its halting circuit until our car hung high in the sky, just short of the summit. Distance obscured the grime and general disrepair of the midway, so the carnival rides looked like glittering toys beneath us.

Lifted far above the blanket of asphalt that held the sun's heat throughout the night, I felt a breeze against my face for the first time in weeks. Cool, it was, with the faint electric scent of ozone.

"Feels like a storm," Finn said.

On the horizon, a band of darker night sky hinted at gathering clouds.

"That would be nice," I said. "Been so dry."

Beneath us, the safety bars clattered and the car gates squeaked as attendants ushered off the last group of riders to make way for the new.

We shared the car with the giant stuffed green elephant Finn had won for me by hurling rings over the necks of old milk bottles with a delicate flick of his wrist. As a result, I didn't have to slide my hand far before I found Finn's fingers. I caressed him softly, and he turned his hand to clasp mine tight, our fingers entwined like teenagers'. The view was magical, but not as wondrous as that moment of closeness. We'd spent the whole evening acting as if we didn't have a care in the world, eating hot dogs and funnel cakes, riding the rides, listening to the bluegrass band playing in the amphitheater.

Now sated, exhausted, and holding my man's hand in my own, I closed my eyes and sighed softly, content if only for an instant.

"Tally?"

"Hmm?"

"These last few months have been . . . incredible."

I felt a smile creep across my face, and I gave his hand a gentle squeeze.

"I don't want this to end," he said.

I cocked one eye open. "Why would it end?"

"It won't." He turned his face forward, not looking squarely at me, and I saw a ripple of uncertainty pass over his features: a slight furrowing of the brow, and thinning of the lips. Finn, usually so glib and carefree, seemed positively tongue-tied. "I mean, that's what I'm trying to say. I want to make sure it won't end."

A curious lightness invaded my limbs as I tried to puzzle out what he was saying.

Out of the corner of my eye, I caught a flicker of

lightning in the distance. And then my stupid phone rang, the William Tell Overture tinkling into the silence between us.

I fumbled in my purse until I found it, glanced at the screen: Bree. I rejected the call. Indictment be damned. Bree could wait.

When I looked up, Finn was watching me, a smoldering heat in his shadowy green eyes. Whatever uncertainty he'd been feeling must have melted away, because even in the half-light I could see a rock-solid resolve in his face. My breath caught.

"I was so angry when I left Dalliance all those years ago. I drove all night, blaring Nine Inch Nails on my cassette player. But then I stopped the next morning in Memphis, got a cup of coffee and watched the sun come up, and I thought, 'Oh, hell, what have I done?'" He smiled his crooked smile, and a gust of wind—redolent of rain—ruffled the swoosh of hair that fell across his forehead. "I spent two days in Memphis, touring Graceland and eating barbecue and trying to decide whether I should come back."

My phone rang again. "Dang it," I muttered.

This time I flipped open the phone.

"Tal—"

"Not now, Bree. Seriously."

"But, Tal—" I flipped the phone shut.

"Sorry."

He waved off my apology. "What I'm trying to say is that I always wondered if leaving that night was the biggest mistake of my life."

I felt a bubble of joy welling up in my chest.

"But now I know it was exactly the right thing to do."

The bubble burst.

"Oh," I said. I mean, what else can you say when your boyfriend tells you he's glad he dumped you? Or, worse, glad that you dumped him. I pulled my hand back into my own lap.

"Tally." Finn's fingers stroked the soft skin beneath my jaw, forcing me to tip my head up to look at him.

"Tally, I had to leave you, be away all those years, so I could grow up. And I had to miss you like crazy so I could appreciate having you back in my life. I loved you then, but what I feel for you now is so much more. So much better."

Beneath us, the Ferris wheel stuttered to life, shifting us slowly up and over the apogee of the arc. Another blast of wind, cool and wet, set the car swinging gently. As we moved through space, I gripped Finn's hand again, held it tighter.

It felt as if something had shaken loose in my chest. As if maybe I'd been holding my breath since the minute I saw Finn Harper sitting on my front porch the year before, and now I could finally exhale. As if the dam of emotion I'd built was going to break with the weather.

"This thing between us," he said, "it's the real deal. I love you."

"I love you, too," I said. But my words came out on a breathy sigh, and I couldn't be sure he heard me over the calliope chaos of the fair below, the grinding of the wheel's gears, and a distant rumble of thunder.

The Ferris wheel cleared the top of its cycle and then stopped again to allow another group of passengers to board.

"Tally, maybe this is crazy, and maybe we should wait. But I'm through with waiting. Life's so short, and when you know what you want . . ." His voice trailed off, and I saw his throat move as he swallowed hard. "I know what I want. I want you."

He raised our clasped hands to his lips and kissed my fingertips, one by one. Then he looked me square in the eye, a question in his gaze. He opened his mouth—

—and my phone, still resting on my knee, rang again. Without thinking, I glanced down to turn it off. This time, the screen told me it was Alice calling.

A million ugly possibilities flitted through my mind at once. The A-la-mode had burned down. Sonny had killed Bree. Bree had killed Sonny. Bree had been arrested . . . again.

"Oh, sugar," I cussed. I glanced at Finn, an apology in my eyes. "Alice. It might be an emergency."

A rueful smile tipped one corner of his mouth. "It's all right. You and your family are a package deal. That's one of the things I love about you."

I flipped open the phone. "This better be good, Alice."

"Tally, this is really important."

I sighed. "Dang it, Bree, I told you I was busy. Can't I have just five minutes here? We're sort of in the middle of something."

"You and Finn?"

"Yes," I hissed. "Something real important."

She was quiet for just a beat, and when she spoke again I heard something in her voice, a thread of despair I'd never heard from Bree before.

"Tally, I got the DNA results today." Of course, the courier that afternoon with his supersecret, superimportant envelope. "I stared at that envelope for hours before I could bring myself to open it." She paused, but from her tone and urgency, I could already guess what she'd say next.

"Sonny isn't Alice's daddy."

"Oh. Oh my. Bree, how's that possible? Who else could it be?"

Beside me, Finn quirked a brow in question. I mouthed "D-N-A."

He grew very still, and he nearly crushed my hand in his grip. I knew he was thinking what I was: not only would this drive a wedge between Bree and Alice, but it would add fuel to the prosecution's case against Bree for Kristen's murder. It wasn't just shame that made Bree mad at Kristen. She legitimately had something to hide.

"Tally," Bree said. "There's something I have to tell you."

I felt my heart grow cold at the gravity of her tone. For an instant, I thought maybe she did it. Maybe she killed Kristen to protect her secret. Maybe she was about to confess.

As quickly as the thought popped into my head, it fled. Bree might be a bit irresponsible and a whole lot of trouble, but she'd never do anything so hurtful or dishonest. Never.

"Tally, you have to believe me. I didn't sleep with anyone after I met Sonny, I swear. I really thought Sonny was Alice's daddy."

"Of course you did."

"But now that I know he isn't, well, I guess the doctors must have been wrong. Alice must have been conceived in May, not June. She wasn't premature, just tiny."

She paused again, but I let her work through whatever she was working through. I knew there was more, and she'd tell it in her own time.

She made a choked sound. If I didn't know Bree better, I'd have sworn it was a sob.

"Tally, I only slept with one guy in the months before I met Sonny. A month before I met Sonny, actually. The night after your wedding. There's only one other person who might be Alice's father."

"Who?"

"Tally, I'm so sorry. The only person it could possibly be is Finn."

At that moment a gust of wind blew across the fairgrounds, rocking the car in which we sat and jarring my hand from Finn's. I looked at him across the handful of inches that separated us, saw the resignation in his eyes. The sadness.

He knew what Bree had told me.

I had a sudden image of Finn the first night he'd returned to Dalliance the year before, the night he showed up on my front porch. In my mind, I saw again the subtle widening of his eyes, the look of barely contained shock on his face, when he first saw Alice.

Had he suspected even then? Had something in the slant of her cheekbones or the angle of her jaw resonated with him on some elemental level?

I felt the phone slide from my fingers, heard it clatter on the floor of the Ferris wheel car, but I couldn't move.

And that was when the storm hit, a crack of lightning striking close. At that moment, the lights went out in Dalliance, plunging the fairgrounds in darkness and stranding me at the top of the Ferris wheel with the one person I wanted most to flee from.

# chapter 17

It took twenty minutes for us to get off that Ferris wheel. And the minute my feet hit the puddles forming on the ride's platform, I hightailed it across the fairgrounds.

I raced through the parking lot, but skidded to a stop when I saw Bree leaning against the side of the van. The sepia-tinted light from an overhead streetlamp turned her hair a mellow copper, and when she raised her head at my approach, the light deepened the shadows around her eyes.

"Not now, Bree."

"Tally, please. I'm so sorry."

"Sorry? Some stuff, sorry doesn't cover."

"I didn't mean to hurt you," she pleaded. "We were both drunk."

I laughed, a sharp and ugly sound echoed by a crack

of thunder overhead. "There it is. The cheater's hat trick—'I'm sorry,' 'Didn't mean to,' and 'I was drunk.' You take lessons from Wayne?" Invoking my tom cat of an ex-husband wasn't really fair, but I didn't care much about fair at that moment.

The barb hit its mark. Bree drew herself up. Even without her high heels, she had a couple of inches on me. She took a step in my direction, forcing me to tip my head back to look her in the eye, but I didn't back down.

"Cheater?" she snapped. "Who were we cheating on? Finn and I were both free agents."

"On me! You were cheating on me! Breaking my heart by screwing around. You knew I loved him, Bree."

"Sure. Loved him so much you dumped him and married another man. Remember that? You had just promised to love, honor, and obey someone else, Tally. Were your vows nothing but lies?"

"Of course not."

"Well, you can't have it both ways. You chose Wayne over Finn. Your choice, Tally. No one else's."

"You think I don't know that?"

She narrowed her eyes. "Of course you do. And that's why you're so mad at me. You made a choice, and now you know it was the wrong one."

"Yeah, well, you made a choice, too. You chose your own libido over everything we'd shared. Like all our history, yours and mine and mine and Finn's, didn't matter a lick compared with a few minutes of mindless pleasure."

Bree staggered back, collapsing against the side of the van as though I'd physically attacked her. I felt a stab of pain as a flash of lightning illuminated the raw anguish on her face.

"That's not fair," she said, the fight gone out of her.

"Nothing about this is fair," I snapped.

I turned on my heel and ran off as fast as my legs would carry me. By the time I made it to the entrance to the parking lot, the skies had opened up again. Billowing sheets of warm water fell to the ground, instantly soaking me to the skin.

Fairgoers shrieked and laughed as they fled the storm and a flood of cars bottlenecked at the entrance to the lot. I moved between them, peering through windshields and searching for a familiar face, until I finally hitched a ride home with some guy I barely recognized, someone I'd seen at the Bar None a time or two.

At home, I made my way to the tiny first-floor room we'd turned into a cozy TV den, wrapped myself in one of Peachy's old quilts, turned off my cell phone, and hunkered down to brood.

I heard Alice traipse in around midnight, her step unmistakably heavy for such a little thing. She stomped up the stairs and slammed into her room. I didn't know if Bree had told her about the paternity results. Even if she had, I didn't have the emotional resources to help her. I knew I'd end up feeding into her anger rather than soothing it.

Peachy and Bree both came in a bit later. They each took a turn at the door to the den, calling my name, but I didn't answer. I wanted to be alone with my pain.

While the storm raged outside, I seethed quietly inside. I spent the night curled on the couch watching ShopNet on the television, Sherbet perched on my hip, occasionally making biscuits on my thigh. Usually the mindless patter of the shopping channel hosts drowned out the babble of my own anxious thoughts and allowed me to drift off to sleep. But that night, all the leather handbags and porcelain collectibles and mineral makeup in the world couldn't silence my bitter internal monologue.

Finally, the storm broke, and as the first hint of dawn brightened the living room window, I nudged Sherbet to the floor and made my way to the front porch and stretched out flat on the swing. The storm had carried in a wall of cool air even more welcome than the rain. I tipped my head back to allow the mild breeze access to my throat as I stared up through the frame of the swing's chains.

Very little grew in our yard. The Texas climate is not naturally conducive to green lawns and ornamental plants, and we didn't have the time or the money to bend the vegetation to our will. The one plant that seemed to thrive was the cherry laurel at the corner of the house. From the street, the elegant emerald leaves and the graceful arc of the small tree's trunk appeared vital. But from my vantage point, I could see a tracery of bare limbs, the fine net of twigs left naked by the plant's instinctive allocation of energy to the branches in the sun.

I gazed into that brittle web and let my eyes go unfocused.

The front screen door opened with the soft whine of unoiled hinges and slapped shut.

"I thought I heard you stirring," Peachy said.

"Didn't sleep."

"It was that kind of night."

She tapped me on the knee, so I swung up into a sitting position. She joined me on the swing's terry cloth cushion.

"This family needs you to hold it together."

"I'm not sure I'm strong enough, Gram."

"*All* my girls are strong. Just how I raised 'em."

I snorted. "I'm not like Bree. Or even Alice. I'm not that tough."

Peachy hummed a little assent. "You're right about that. That's a good thing. See, all that independence has a downside. The Decker girls make dumb-ass mistakes, are too proud to admit it, and way too proud to ask for help. You're just a little softer than the rest of us, Tally. Soft enough to bend without breaking."

"I don't know," I hedged.

"I do. Now, you had your little pity party, and you were entitled. Today, you have to put your big girl pants on and help Alice through this."

I cut my eyes to the side to see Peachy's face. "Bree told her?"

"Of course. I made her do it. Told her Alice deserved to be the first person to know." Peachy frowned. "Alice pitched a royal fit. But she understands that this hurts her mother's legal situation pretty bad. If the authorities find out Bree really had something to hide—that Sonny was right to challenge his paternity of Alice—then it seems even more plausible she would kill to keep it quiet. I told her she needs to keep her mouth shut for now, and she gets it."

Peachy patted my knee again. "Look at me, Tallulah."

I did as she ordered, turning my head to face my grandma. The diffuse morning light blended away some of the lines in her face, softened her, but there was no mistaking the rock-hard resolve in her eyes.

"The same goes for you, my child. You, Alice, Bree, and I know about those DNA results—"

"And Finn. He was with me when Bree called."

Peachy's mouth tightened at the corners. "Well, the five of us are the only folks in Dalliance who know that Sonny isn't Alice's daddy. And it's going to stay that way until we get this murder charge against your cousin dropped. You hear?"

"Yes'm."

"That means you and Finn Harper are going to keep on keepin' on, just as lovey-dovey as you have been. No one's going to suspect a thing."

The thought of spending time with Finn, maintaining a pretense that all was well, made me die a little inside. But I'd been raised to do what Peachy said.

"Yes'm."

"Huh." Peachy laughed, a rasping deep in her smoker's lungs. "I see that look in your eyes. You want to give that boy what-for. Well, if you want a big blowout with Finn Harper, you better set your mind to getting Bree out of trouble. The sooner you get her off the hook, the sooner you can rip him a new one."

Peachy was right. My relationship with Finn was definitely in jeopardy, and I wasn't a hundred percent sure I could ever trust Bree again. But I loved my family—Bree included—and I knew we'd never recover if Bree went to prison for killing Kristen. The DNA results were another nail in Bree's coffin, evidence that Bree had a strong incentive to put the kibosh on the lawsuit, and I needed to start prying up some boards if I was going to save us all.

# chapter 18

I decided to start with the one person who seemed to want to talk about Kristen: Neck DeWinter.

He scared the ever-living bejesus out of me, but Neck seemed legitimately broken up about Kristen's death, and I figured maybe he would be willing to open up about her life a bit.

When I'm right, I'm right.

After a quick call to Jason Arbaugh, I had no trouble tracking Neck to the Bar None. He was slouched over a pint of something that looked more like blackstrap molasses than beer. Even at midday, the interior of the Bar None was dim, but Neck's eyes were hidden behind his shades.

"Can I join you?" I asked, half hoping he'd say no.

He nodded sullenly.

"How are you holding up, Neck?"

He took a pull on his beer by way of answer.

"That bad, huh? Would it help to talk about her?"

His beefy shoulders inched up. Was that a yes?

"How long did you know Kristen?"

He sighed. "I didn't meet her in person until two years ago. Best day of my life."

"In person? Did you meet her online before that?"

He laughed, a short, brittle bark. "Huh. Yeah, I did."

I didn't see what was so funny about meeting her online. I was pretty old-school, but I knew lots of folks who'd used online dating services. Some of them even ended up marrying the people they met.

"She was so beautiful," he said, a river of raw ache running through his voice.

"She certainly was. I heard she had a mess of crowns from the pageants she won."

He tilted his head slightly to the side. I really wished I could read his eyes, but the movement made me think I'd confused him a bit.

"The crowns?"

"Yeah, crowns from beauty pageants. Those are tough to come by."

"eBay."

I know I'm not brilliant like Alice, but I fancy myself reasonably intelligent. But talking to Neck, I felt like an idiot. He was saying words—I heard them come out of his mouth—and they were English words, but I couldn't make heads nor tails of them. Not at all.

"Excuse me?" I said, trying to keep the thread of annoyance out of my voice.

"eBay. Those crowns are easy to find on eBay."

"But, I mean, the titles. Those are hard to come by."

"She deserved more," he said. "She won runner-up for Miss Am-Cam in 1995, but she was the best. The most beautiful ever."

It occurred to me then that Neck was loaded. It was only eleven forty-five in the morning, and he was steady as a rock as he sat in his booth, but he was totally tanked. That was the only way I could explain his lack of coherence. After all, Cookie had said Kristen had lots of pageant titles, including some big one. Miss American Spirit? No, Miss American Pride. But Neck was acting as if Kristen had only been an also-ran.

I took a deep breath to steel my nerves and reached across to pat his hand gently.

"I'm real sorry for your loss, Neck," I said. "If you ever want to talk more, you just let me know."

I scooted back to the A-la-mode, where I found Kyle manning the store, sitting on my lovely marble counter, kicking his dirty sneakers against the polished oak wainscoting.

"Down," I ordered. "And where is everyone?"

He slid off the counter without a fuss. "Beth took her kid clothes shopping. Grandma and Bree are at the fairgrounds. Alice went off to have lunch with Mr. Harper."

If Kyle thought it was weird that Alice and Finn had a lunch date, he didn't let on.

My own response to the news was tough to untangle. On the one hand, Alice had never had a dad before. Now she had one, and he was, at heart, a good man. She deserved an opportunity to build a relationship with him. But, selfishly, I felt a stab of anxiety at the notion of Finn having a permanent seat at the family table, whether I liked it or not. Or, worse, Finn, Alice, and Bree building some sort of nuclear family . . . one that didn't include me.

It was out of my hands, though. Peachy's reminder that I needed to put on my big girl pants echoed in my mind, and I mentally shook it off.

"Kyle, my boy, do you have your laptop with you?"

"Always."

Kyle was a troublemaker with a capital *T*, but we'd learned that he had a very definite skill set. Specifically, he had an encyclopedic knowledge of sports statistics and an amazing ability with computers, both to dig around in the guts of the machines themselves and to use the machines to navigate the vast network of digital information called the Internet.

"And can you still get online through McKlesky and Howard's network?"

At the beginning of the summer, we'd also discovered that the law firm next door didn't have its Wi-Fi network password-protected. I maintained that using their network without their permission was a form of stealing, but I'd been labeled "old-fashioned" and "out of touch" and "downright backward" by everyone else . . . Kyle, Alice, Bree, Finn, and even Grandma Peachy (who liked to play euchre online).

Kyle was pulling his beat-up laptop out of its equally beat-up case. "We can still surf for free. You need me to look something up?"

"Yeah. I want you to look up the Miss American Pride Pageant."

Kyle snorted. "You thinking of entering."

"No, smarty-pants. I'm not. Just hush up and do what I tell you."

"Yes, ma'am."

His fingers flew over his keyboard in a crazed sort of hunt-and-peck, the savantlike movements of someone who'd never been taught to type but was remarkably well self-taught.

"Miss American Pride," he said. "Held every April in Missoula, Montana."

Montana? I thought Kristen was from Galveston. But maybe girls from all over the country could enter.

"Is there a list of winners?"

"Uh-huh."

I tried to remember when Cookie said Kristen had won. Sometime in the early 2000s.

"Read me the winners starting in, say, 1997."

Kyle heaved a put-upon sigh, but he obliged. "Nineteen ninety-seven—Anna Hooper. Ninety-eight—Marie Cavendish. Ninety-nine—Tonya Ortiz. Two thousand—Cindy Lou Phillips. Cindy Lou? Really?"

"No editorializing. Just read."

"Two thousand one—Megan Tyler. Two thousand two—Alisha Thomas. Two thousand three—Ashley Tyler. I wonder if Ashley and Megan are sisters." He sounded a bit wistful at the notion of sibling beauty queens.

"No Kristen Ver Steeg?"

"Kristen? No. Maybe she was a runner-up?"

I didn't think so. A runner-up wouldn't have a crown.

"Check," I said. "And look for anyone named Kristen. Maybe she had a marriage somewhere in there, her name changed."

Kyle's fingers danced across the keys. "Only Kristen I see was a second runner-up in 1989. Here's her picture."

He turned the laptop around so I could see the screen. A color picture filled the screen, a young woman with a freakishly white smile, a spiral perm, and a poofy hot-pink taffeta dress. Definitely not Kristen Ver Steeg, who would have been in middle school in 1989.

I was pretty sure Cookie had said the Miss American Pride crown was from 2001, the year Megan Tyler— one of the beauty queen sisters—won the title. So how did Kristen get the crown?

Then it clicked.

"eBay."

"What?" Kyle asked.

"Can you see stuff that used to be on eBay? Like stuff that sold a while ago?"

"Sure," Kyle said. "Once something's on the Internet, it's basically just out there. Forever."

I didn't want to stop to think too much about that horrifying thought. "See if you can find a listing for a Miss American Pride crown on eBay."

He started typing again, and then paused. "Are we investigating a murder?"

"Officially? Like what you tell your mama? No, we're indulging your boss's idle curiosity. But off the books, yeah, we're investigating a murder."

A smug smile spread across his face. "Cool."

He tapped away for a while, and finally said, "Got it. The 2001 Miss American Pride crown sold last year, in November, for thirty-two fifty. Picture's total crap, by the way."

"Let me guess. Kristen Ver Steeg won the auction?"

"Ms. Tally, people don't use their real names on eBay. But I don't think Kristen won the auction. The person used the handle 'Wildcatter-ninety.' "

Wildcatter. As in the Dalliance High School Wildcatters, maybe? And 1990 was the year ahead of me. Neck DeWinter's year.

The picture that was forming broke my heart: Neck DeWinter, big oaf, buying secondhand pageant crowns for his own personal beauty queen.

Jeez.

There was just one nagging little detail I wanted to check out. Neck had said Kristen did place in one pageant.

"Okay. One more search, kiddo. Miss Am-Cam."

"Is that all one word? Like the name of a town?"

I hoped so, because maybe it would give us a better sense of where Kristen came from. "I'm not sure. Use your imagination."

While Kyle typed, I fetched us each a can of soda from the back. By the time I returned to the front of the store, Kyle had his laptop closed and his face had drained of color.

"What's up?" I asked, alarmed by the freaked-out expression on his face.

"Just remember, you asked me to look this up, right? It's not my fault."

"What's not your fault?"

Kyle pried up the lid of his laptop, waking it up. Immediately, the sound of moaning and panting filled the air.

"Sweet Jesus. What is that?"

Mortified color suffused Kyle's face. "I'm not a hundred percent sure, but I think it's the clip that won Miss Am-Cam 2009 her title."

"Excuse me?"

"Miss Am-Cam is Miss Amateur Camera. It's, uh, an award for homemade Internet porn."

I was torn. On the one hand, I definitely wanted more information now. On the other hand, I didn't feel good about using Kyle to get it. I mean, he was technically an adult, almost nineteen, but still . . .

"First, can you turn the sound off on your computer?"

"Yes, ma'am." He scrambled to comply.

"Okay, is there some way you can get a list of, uh, winners? Without cuing any more videos," I rushed to add.

"Yes, ma'am."

With his eyes studiously on his keyboard, only glancing at the screen ever so briefly, Kyle poked around.

"Here's a list of the winners and runners-up for the last twenty years, since the contest was created."

Neck had said Kristen was runner-up in 1995. "Look at 1995."

"Um, oh, jeez." Kyle cleared his throat and sat up a little straighter, clearly trying to be adult about this. "The winner was someone named . . . Here." He spun the computer around so I could read the screen, then shoved away from the table and grabbed his soda. "I'm gonna do the dishes," he said as he popped the top on his can.

I let him go and looked at the list. The names were, um, colorful. Clearly not the names these young women had been christened with.

Oh my.

The runner-up was not listed as Kristen Ver Steeg, but I recognized her face in the still shot next to the name. Either the lighting was really bad or her hair was darker, the color of English toffee. But the delicate lines of her face were unmistakable, even though they were contorted in a very unladylike expression.

Next to her pseudonym and the still shot, there was a short bio line. *This Lonestar lovely gives a whole new meaning to the phrase "deep in the heart of Texas." Want more? Catch her IRL at the Pony Up Gentlemen's Club.*

"Kyle," I yelled.

"What?"

"What does I-R-L mean?"

"In real life," he shouted back.

The text of the club name was in another color, and I knew that meant it was a link to another Web site. With a good deal of trepidation, I used the laptop's track pad to guide the cursor over the link, and then pressed it.

Turns out the Pony Up was right up the road in Fort Worth. A strip club.

The bits of information were flying through my mind at a dizzying speed. The Kristen Ver Steeg I'd met had been pristine, icy, professional. But apparently she came from more humble beginnings, making a living stripping and performing sex acts on the Internet.

Proving once again that people were rarely what they seemed to be.

# chapter 19

I tried to leave all thought of Kirsten and her sordid past behind when I made my pilgrimage to the fairgrounds that afternoon. But it seemed as if everywhere I turned, I ran into another reminder of Kristen and her murder.

It started when I went to get supper.

"Three chef's salads. I've got a pint for each of them."

The curly-haired girl working the Prickly Pear Café's fair booth looked over her shoulder to silently consult with her two college-age colleagues. The other two girls each nodded, and the curly-haired one turned back to me, her eyes narrowed as though she were far more shrewd than her button-bedecked vest would lead one to believe.

"Deal," she said.

I handed over the cooler containing three pints of

the A-la-mode's ice cream, my part of our hastily arranged barter agreement, then found a chair beneath their meager awning to await my order.

The mood in the A-la-mode booth at the fairgrounds had been tense all afternoon. Bree and I circled each other like a couple of wary cats, and Alice periodically broke down in tears for no apparent reason. I suppose it would have been more practical to keep us all separated for a bit longer, but Kyle needed to spend a few hours with his family; Peachy had met up with a gaggle of women from Tarleton Ranch for a tour of the fair's quilt exhibit; and Beth didn't have a babysitter, so she had to work in the store, where she could keep an eye on her child.

When dinnertime rolled around, I eagerly volunteered to go get us all some food. Bree had begged for something that hadn't been deep-fried, as she was taking the stage later in the evening for the much-anticipated karaoke competition. She didn't want a bloat when she squeezed into her tight black satin capris to sing "Before He Cheats."

I had just taken a deep breath when someone tapped me on my shoulder.

I turned in my seat to find Jason Arbaugh and his wife, Crystal, Deena's daughter. Jason held Crystal tight around the waist and she leaned into him, snuggling despite the return of the oppressive heat.

"Hey, kids," I said. Technically, I was still a little young to be a mom to the twenty-five-year-old Jason, but both he and Crystal were firmly on the other side of a generational divide. "Enjoying the fair?"

"Trying to," Jason said with a wistful smile. "It's

about as close to a night on the town as we're gonna get for a while."

"Still no luck finding a permanent job?" I guessed.

"Ha! At this point, no job at all," he said.

Crystal bonked her head against his shoulder. "You did the right thing, leaving." Her soft features glowed as she stared up into his face, alight with the unquestioning adoration of young love.

"You quit Jackson and Ver Steeg?" I asked.

Jason rolled his lips between his teeth. "Yeah. Things around there were getting . . . weird."

"Weird how?"

"It's complicated."

"Do you mean, 'it's privileged'?" I asked.

He shrugged.

"No," Crystal said, giving her spouse a meaningful look. "It's not. What's in the files is privileged. What Maddie asked you to do with the files is not."

"What do you mean?"

Jason looked uncomfortable. "Maddie asked me to start shredding a bunch of old client files."

"What's wrong with that?"

"Nothing, technically. But she wasn't clearing out all the old files, just, uh, some of them."

I thought about the note that had fallen out of Neck's pocket with the list of names Finn had identified as drug dealers. On a hunch, I asked, "Were they all drug cases?"

"That . . . that *would* be privileged information," Jason stammered, but the look of near panic on his face told me I'd hit the nail on the head.

"Huh," I said casually. "Did Jackson and Ver Steeg represent a lot of drug dealers?"

Jason's expression turned to one of confusion. "No. No dealers. Just petty users." He winced. "Alleged. Alleged petty users."

Now, that *was* weird. Why would Maddie be shredding the files for a bunch of possession cases, while Neck was walking around with a list of three of the biggest dealers in town in his pocket? It didn't add up.

Something hinky was happening at Kristen's law firm, and it might have something to do with her death, but darned if I could figure out what it might be. As much as it pained me to contemplate, I decided I should probably call Finn and get his take on the information.

While I had Jason there, though, I decided to do a little more fishing. "I heard that Kristen was a stickler for the rules," I said, quoting back Cookie Milhone's description almost verbatim. "I can't imagine she'd be involved in anything unethical."

"Kristen?" Jason said. "I guess I never really thought of her that way. But, now that you mention it, she did file a question with the state ethics board just a few weeks ago."

"Wait. Kristen filed an ethics question?"

"I . . . Wow. I think I should really not say anything else," Jason said. His face had turned bright pink, and he actually took a step back.

I felt a pang of guilt. Poor kid. Here he was, brand-new to his profession, and I'd been trying to trick him into offering more information than he should.

"Sorry, Jason," I said. "I'll let you two get back to your date."

As I watched them walk away, her hand in his back pocket, I tried to process what I'd learned. Deena had been under the impression that Jason had raised ethical concerns about his employers. But if Kristen had been the one with problems . . . maybe whatever hinky things Maddie was doing at the law firm had bothered Kristen enough that she'd brought in the authorities. I was feeling more and more as though those shredded files might have something to do with Kristen's death.

"Got your salads, Miss Jones." The curly-haired girl set my cooler on the counter.

I smiled. When you're strapped for cash, barter is a pretty fantastic way to do business.

And that's when it hit me . . . I thought maybe, just maybe, I knew what was going on at Jackson and Ver Steeg.

I'd made it halfway back to the A-la-mode booth when I ran smack into Sonny Anders.

"Oh, for the love of . . ."

"Good to see you, too, Tally."

He was channeling his inner Johnny Cash, with a black suit, silver-tipped black boots, and a ridiculously clean black cowboy hat. Judging by the nice duds and the scent of some high-end cologne wafting off him, I guessed he was on his way to bilk some more people out of their money. Or to bilk some girl out of her panties. One or the other.

"No offense, Sonny, but you're pretty much the last person I want to talk to right now."

"Now, is that any way to treat a member of the family?"

"You're not family anymore, remember? Bree divorced you."

He rocked back on his heels. "We still got blood in common."

I opened my mouth to snap back, but then clamped it shut. Dang it all, when this whole mess had started, Sonny was the bad guy trying to disown Alice. Now the tables were turned. The Decker girls had lost the moral high ground, and now Sonny was the one in the dark, unaware that he really wasn't Alice's daddy.

Still, I reminded myself, he was a no-account snake in the grass who left his wife and the child he *thought* was his own high and dry to run off with a stripper. And now he was ripping off my friends and neighbors. He didn't deserve my pity.

I'm not proud of it, but I was confused and conflicted . . . and I resorted to playground tactics. "You're a sleaze."

He grinned. "Nice one, Tally. Clever."

"About as clever as your oil scam. How's that going?"

He *tsk*ed softly. "Now, Tallulah, that there is dangerously close to slander. I'm just offering some intrepid businessmen the opportunity to partner with me in a legitimate corporate enterprise."

"Uh-huh. An opportunity to pour their money into your pockets. And how much of it will they get back?"

He shrugged. "There are risks associated with every business. I assure you everything I'm doing is one hundred percent legal."

"Maybe. But there's what's legal and there's what's right. And they're not necessarily the same thing. Speaking of legal, have you found another attorney to represent you? Someone to help you persecute Bree and create a legal shield for your oil 'investment'?" I was holding the cooler in one hand, so I could only make one-half of the air quotes, but my sarcasm was pretty obvious.

His smile faltered a bit. "We're working on that."

"You mean not every lawyer is champing at the bit to help you con people out of their cash?"

I was talking faster than I was thinking, but my brain was catching up. Jason had just said that Kristen had filed an ethics question with some state agency. Maybe Kristen had reservations about helping Sonny with his scam. Alice had seen Sonny with Kristen at the Dutch Oven the night before she was killed. If she had told him about her ethical concerns, maybe he was afraid she was going to blow the whistle on him. Maybe he'd killed her to protect his con. If he was willing to drag his own child through hell and back to save himself a few bucks, surely he wasn't above killing a veritable stranger for the same.

I narrowed my eyes and fixed Sonny with a hard look. "Did Kristen have a problem with the oil deal? Was she getting cold feet?"

Never let it be said that Sonny Anders is a stupid man. Vain, amoral, and even a little lazy. But not stupid.

He cottoned to where I was going right away.

"Whoa," he said, raising his hands in defense. "Hold on just a second. I didn't have any reason in the world to kill Kristen. First, she didn't draft the incorporation papers for the oil deal."

Of course not. Duh. Why would he need lawyers to draft incorporation papers for a corporation that wasn't even real?

"She was just representing me in the paternity suit," he continued. "And as far as I know, she was happy as a clam to be representing us. I only met her like twice, ever. Char retained her, and Char never said word one about Kristen having a problem with our lawsuit."

He cleared his throat. "We'd contacted Kristen weeks before we got to Dalliance, and she had the papers all drawn up before we even arrived. Billed us a pretty penny for her work, too. I was the one who hesitated to pull the trigger and actually file the dang thing."

It might sound crazy, since I knew Sonny to be a bald-faced liar, but I believed him. I'd caught him off guard, and even Sonny couldn't spin a yarn that fast.

Besides, I was sure I saw a flash of genuine emotion on his face, some real sorrow. He looked past me. "She was better off without me."

"Who? Alice?"

He nodded.

I couldn't bring myself to argue with him.

He coughed, as if he was choking back tears. "She grew so much. Got herself a boy, I hear."

"Yep."

"God, I remember being that young." He nodded

toward something behind me, and I turned to see two kids wrapped around each other in a heated embrace. They were half in the shadows, but I could make out the boy's head, shaved on both sides in a style only a teenager could get away with. And when they shifted just so, the girl's long hair fell away from her face, and I realized it was Dani Carberry.

"That's how I felt when I met Bree, you know."

"It didn't last, though, did it?"

"What do you mean?"

"Well, you left her. You must have gotten bored with her. The spark died."

He looked at me, a quizzical smile on his face. "Are you kidding me? You think I could get bored with Bree? No way."

"Then why did you leave? Why did you leave her and Alice?"

"Just like I said. They were better off without me."

"But you had a family. You had a home."

He swiped his hat from his head, ran his fingers through his hair, and plopped the hat back on. "Aw, Tally, don't you know? Home is the most dangerous place in the world. Where folks can kill you by inches, or cut out your heart with a single look, just because you love 'em so damn much."

# chapter 20

The karaoke competition didn't start until nine, and Bree had scored the closing spot on the bill by winning a drawing at the Bar None, which was sponsoring the whole shebang. The competition was open to walk-ons, so we didn't know exactly when Bree would go on, but it would certainly be late enough that we could wait for Beth to close up the shop on the square and for her and Kyle to take over the fair booth so the whole family could go watch Bree perform.

"Are you sure I should?" Bree had asked. "I mean maybe it's tacky for me to perform when I'm out on bail for murder."

"Girl, you need to do this," Peachy had insisted. "You didn't kill that woman, and you shouldn't act guilty. You just live your life."

Peachy and I locked arms around her shoulders and

walked with her to the amphitheater, because Lord knows karaoke was Bree's life. To the best of my knowledge, the prospect of fronting a real band—original or cover—had never been a draw for her, but she loved to take to the stage for karaoke. And she was good, voice like a spring songbird's and a gift for working a crowd.

The crowd in the fairground amphitheater rocked, too. It was huge and, truth be told, mostly drunk. They cheered and booed in equal measures, but they got het up about every act that took the stage.

Ted and Shelley Alrecht, Bar None karaoke regulars, were the last act with advance registration to take the mic. During the second verse of their totally predictable "Islands in the Stream," Alice arrived.

With Finn Harper.

"I hope it's okay," Alice said shyly, looking up at me through her long pale lashes. "I know it's weird, but he's family now."

I couldn't find the words to respond.

"Honest, Aunt Tally. He's been trying real hard. We had lunch the other day, and I get it. He didn't know I was his kid. If he had, he would have been here."

With the sheer narcissism of youth, Alice thought Finn's sin was being an absent dad. It never occurred to her that I might have been hurt by the very act of her conception.

I gave her a hug, and glared at Finn over her shoulder.

"What are you doing here?" I hissed, once Alice had drifted out of earshot.

"Well, for one, I'm supporting Alice. She's my . . ." He raked his fingers through his hair. "Dammit. She's my daughter. I still can't quite get used to the idea."

"We're all struggling with that one."

Finn flinched at the poison in my tone. "I know, Tally. But we're supposed to be keeping this turn of events quiet, right? For Bree? And that means we need to keep acting like the happy couple."

As angry as I was with him, his words stung.

"Will that be so hard?"

He hooked his forefinger beneath my chin and tipped my head, forcing me to meet his eyes. "It's not hard for me at all, Tally. If I could undo this . . ."

The play of emotions in his eyes mesmerized me. Regret, hope, grief, joy. I couldn't imagine what it must be like to discover you're a parent. With a single word, the proverbial flip of a switch, to become father to a grown child.

Really, I couldn't. I just couldn't. I couldn't empathize with Finn yet. I still needed time to lick my wounds.

"Let's just get through tonight," I said.

Our bizarre little family unit huddled near the edge of the stage, waiting Bree's turn. Finn stood at my side, close but not quite touching, as the walk-on competitors began performing.

As the umpteenth dude in shit-kickers and a hat took to the stage to belt out Toby Keith's "Courtesy of the Red, White and Blue," Bree turned green.

"I can't do it, Tally. I'm gonna puke."

I took her by the shoulders and looked her in the eye. "You absolutely *can* do this. You *will* do this, if only to show your daughter that everything is okay, that her world is still turning. So if you need to puke before you get up there and sing your heart out, you go right ahead and puke. And then you sing."

Her brow furrowed with resolve, Bree nodded. "Okay. I'm just gonna go vomit."

"Good girl."

But before Bree could take more than a step away, the emcee waved at her, letting her know she was on next.

"Oh, crap," Bree moaned. "I don't have time to hit the Porta Potti. I'm gonna have to puke onstage."

"No, you're not." Finn's hands rested on my shoulders. "We'll buy you a few minutes. You go get sick, then hustle back."

Bree smiled her thanks, then dashed off before I could say a word.

I spun on Finn. "What do you mean, we'll buy her a few minutes?"

"I guess we're going to sing," he said, a devilish glint in his eyes.

"Oh no. I'm not singing. You go right ahead."

"What would people think? It's what couples do, sing karaoke together."

"Not at the fairgrounds in front of thousands of people."

"Chicken."

"Absolutely."

He laughed.

Peachy, who'd been hanging back during this whole conversation, stepped forward. "Both of you quit your bantering and get up on that stage," she snapped. "Right now. That's an order."

When Peachy took that tone, my body obeyed before my mind even knew what hit it. I was halfway to the mic before I realized I didn't even know what we'd be singing. I glanced over my shoulder and saw Finn consulting with the stage manager.

Finn joined me center stage. The crowd fell quiet. I nearly passed out. Finn rested his big warm hand in the small of my back, and I felt stronger.

The music began, and I watched the karaoke video begin to play on the screens set at the foot of the stage. When I recognized the song, I shot Finn a nasty look, but he just smiled down at me.

A beat after the first piano chord sounded, Finn started singing, and soon I was joining in, as the two of us crooned Dan Hill's and Vonda Shepard's parts in "Can't We Try."

By the refrain, the crowd was booing in earnest. Rightly so. We were terrible. Neither of us could hit the notes, and our timing was all off.

I heard them, but I didn't care. In a weird way, Finn and I were talking to each other, our hurt mediated by the neutral arbiter of Dan Hill's lyrics. *Can't we try just a little more passion? Can't we try just a little less pride? I love you so much, baby, that it tears me up inside.*

By the time the song ended, the crowd was close to stoning us. I'd stopped singing, lost in Finn's eyes. He wrapped it up, singing directly to my heart. *Can't we try just a little bit harder? Can't we give just a little bit more?*

He grabbed my hand, and squeezed. For a beat, we just stood there in silence while the crowd voiced its displeasure. For a beat, I thought maybe we'd get past this crisis. If we just tried a little bit harder.

When he lifted my fingers to his lips, I shook myself out of my stupor. I glanced to the side of the stage and saw Bree standing there, waiting to go on, a pained look on her face.

I grinned, a big, stupid grin, and felt a bubble of laughter, relief, rise in my chest. I pulled Finn behind me as I bolted for the far side of the stage, where performers exited. He quickly took the lead, tugging me along in his wake, his own smile a beacon leading me forward.

I was halfway down the steps when I happened to glance toward the crowd and a familiar face caught my eye.

The kid with the funky shaved head, the one who had been molesting Dani Carberry a few hours earlier. Only now his body folded protectively around the form of another girl. One with a haircut similar to his, shaved close on one side, cut in jagged peaks everywhere else, and dyed a brilliant purple. This girl was about as far from Dani's headband-and-khakis all-American look as a girl could get.

Sort of like the way Bree's bodacious, flamboyant sexuality was as far from my own staid, good-girl persona as it could possibly be.

As my foot hit the ground, I pulled my hand out of Finn's.

He looked over his shoulder, and I watched as the giddy smile on his face faded.

Maybe we could try just a little bit harder and make it work. But we hadn't gotten there yet.

Later that night, we opened the A-la-mode for an impromptu celebration of Bree's big karaoke win. She'd slain the audience with her Carrie Underwood cover, whipping them into a frenzy as she belted out the anthem of revenge.

Bree made the milk shakes while Peachy listened with good-natured interest to Alice's detailed postmortem of the performance.

I pulled Finn aside.

"So I've been thinking," I said.

"Always dangerous," he quipped.

"Ha-ha. Seriously, I saw Jason Arbaugh at the fair tonight, and he said something hinky is going down at Jackson and Ver Steeg, and I think I know what it is."

"Do tell."

"Well, Jason sorta slipped up, and he let me know that Maddie is shredding the files of her drug-using clients, the ones who were busted for possession. And she was snapping at Neck about keeping it together, like maybe they had some shady deal going on. And Neck," I said, completing the circle, "was walking around with a list of big-time drug dealers in his pocket."

"So . . . ?"

"Well, we know the firm was strapped for cash. What if the firm had a deal with the dealers? What if Maddie was connecting buyers and sellers, and taking a cut as commission?"

Finn nodded, eyes squinted thoughtfully. "Maybe. But what do the dealers get out of it?"

"Business."

"They've already got business."

"But wouldn't they want more? I mean, Maddie had a steady supply of addicts she could refer to them."

He tipped his head to the side, skeptical.

"Maddie's clients had gotten busted with dope. They had suppliers already. And if the dealers were looking for a list of addicts, they could get the names off the court docket themselves, without risking Maddie and Kristen as middlemen."

He raised an excellent point. But I felt like we were on to something, and I couldn't let it go. "Maddie's up to no good, and it has something to do with dealers and users. I just know it."

"You may be right about the big picture, even if the details are off. Tell you what. I'll do a little digging tomorrow morning, and then you and I can pay Ms. Jackson a visit."

Whether our romantic relationship could be healed or not, one thing was certain: Finn and I made a pretty awesome crime-fighting duo.

# chapter 21

The Law Offices of Jackson and Ver Steeg grew more depressing by the day, it seemed. When Finn and I showed up the next day, Jason was gone, the front desk chair empty, the front desk itself buried beneath an avalanche of unopened mail.

"Hello?" I called.

"Yes?" Maddie hustled into the waiting area, breathing heavy. Her hair was mussed and she had a wicked run in her hose.

She frowned in annoyance when she saw us.

"What do you want?" she snapped.

No wonder Jackson and Ver Steeg was hurting for clients. Maddie didn't have the most winning personality.

Finn inched forward. "We'd like to talk to you about

your client list. You seem to have quite a stable of drug clients."

"I'm a lawyer," Maddie said. "Drug users need lawyers."

"I think it's a little more complicated than that," Finn said. "Maybe we could sit down and discuss it."

Maddie sighed. "Fine. Come on in. Say your piece."

She led us back to the conference room where Deena and I had found Neck. The big guy was nowhere in sight.

"So," Finn said as we all settled in, "I spent a few hours looking at some of your clients' files at the courthouse this morning."

"Really? Nothing better to do?"

"Turns out it made for fascinating reading. Your clients who get busted for possession, they seem to get more time than most. People who get busted for possession, they usually get a walk or a slap on the wrist, as long as they tell the authorities where they got their junk. But your clients . . . your clients are surprisingly discreet. And they pay for their refusal to narc on their dealers with longer, harsher sentences."

"Wow," Maddie said with a sneer. "Thanks for coming all this way to tell me I'm a crappy lawyer. Made my day."

Finn smiled and shook his head. "I don't think you're a crappy lawyer at all. I think you're very shrewd."

Maddie's eyes narrowed, her lips thinned, but she didn't say a word.

"Here's what I think," Finn said, leaning forward to rest his folded arms on the glass-topped table. "I think you've got a little arrangement with Eddie Collins, Juan Solis, and Daniel Skarsgaard, all local dealers. I think you counsel your clients against cooperating with the authorities. You sell out your clients to protect the dealers and, in exchange, the dealers pay you a little commission."

Maddie's expression didn't waver as Finn spoke, but the color drained from her face.

Then she laughed. "Jeez. You guys think I'm some sort of criminal mastermind, huh? That's quite a theory."

Finn shrugged. "It's a little more than a theory. First, your associate, Neck, got a little careless with his notes."

I pulled the crumpled envelope that had fallen out of Neck's pocket from my purse and held it up so Maddie could see it. When she reached to take it from my hand, I pulled it back. As I refolded it and put it back in my purse, securely on my lap, she watched my every move with a venomous gaze.

"There's that," Finn said. "And then I tracked down one of those clients who didn't cooperate. Wiley Bishop."

I confess, I was a little surprised Wiley dallied with drugs. He's always been a hard-core alcoholic, but I didn't think he strayed from the bottle. Apparently, though, old age has brought on some medical issues and Wiley thought maybe a little pot might help.

"I gifted Wiley with a pint of whiskey," Finn continued, "shared a shot or two with him." He glanced at me, smiled his rakish smile. "It was after noon, I promise. And I used my own cup." He turned his attention back to Maddie. "After a couple of drinks, I asked Wiley about getting busted. I asked him how he chose his lawyer. Wiley told me something interesting."

Maddie's nostrils flared.

"Wiley said the guy who sold him the pot actually gave him your business card along with the weed." Finn leaned back in his chair. "That's quite a referral system."

I could see the wheels turning behind Maddie's eyes.

"Still just speculation. I mean, let's say—hypothetically, of course—you're right. My communications with my clients are privileged. No way for anyone to know what was said."

"Except your partner," I said. "Kristen would have known. Especially since Neck, the resident ex-con and all-around badass, was making the connections for you, and Neck was tail-over-teakettle in love with Kristen."

"Hypothetically." Maddie nodded. "Hypothetically, she might have had some knowledge of how I advised my clients. So? My privilege extends to her."

I decided to stop dancing with the woman. "Look, we know Kristen filed an ethics question with the state bar."

Maddie looked puzzled. Then she smiled again. "Oh, I see. You think Kristen was troubled by our business practices. And you think . . . wow. You think I killed Kristen?"

Actually, no, we didn't think Maddie killed Kristen. At least not personally. Maddie was a hefty woman who got winded trotting down her office hallway. No way she managed to get herself up onto the saloon girl's balcony and then get down and out before Cal and I rushed the joint.

"Maybe," I hedged. "Prove to us you didn't."

Maddie grinned. "This is what us lawyers call a 'fishing expedition.' You're just bluffing your way through this, hoping to get information out of me."

She clasped her hands together and leaned forward. "Why don't you just ask me what you want to ask me? I didn't kill my partner. In fact, her dying leaves me in a bit of a bind. She had the better clients, the ones who actually paid their bills. And she was sort of my friend. I didn't want her dead."

Sort of her friend, but not entirely. It seemed to me there was some wiggle room in that statement. Enough to rationalize a murder?

"So, if you didn't want her dead, who did?" I asked.

She shrugged. "I don't know. If I had to put money on someone, though, I'd put it on Tucker Gentry."

"Tucker? Why? Because of the lawsuit?"

She nodded appreciatively. "So you know about the suit. I'm impressed."

"Just that it exists," Finn said. "We don't know who was suing him or why. You want to enlighten us?"

"Uh, no. Privilege, remember?"

"Really? You're going to hide behind legal ethics?"

She shrugged again. "Let's just say that, hypothetically, I'm turning over a new leaf. You want to know what the lawsuit is about, ask Tucker."

"What makes you think he wanted Kristen dead?" I asked. "Can you at least tell us that?"

She closed her eyes, thinking, and then heaved herself to her feet. She left the room for a few seconds, returning with a small digital recorder in her hand.

"He's not our client, so his communications with us are not privileged," she explained. "He left this message on our voice mail two weeks ago."

She pressed the button on the recording device and Tucker's voice filled the room, resonant with hellfire and brimstone. "Miss Ver Steeg, you are doing the devil's own work. I urge you to tend to your eternal soul."

Maddie clicked the recorder. "The rest of the message contained references to our client. This is the part we pulled out to give to the cops."

"You gave this to the police?" Finn asked.

"When we got it. They filed a report but didn't seem to think it was any big deal."

I wondered if the officers who had filed the report had bothered to tell the officers investigating Kristen's death about the implied threat.

"Talk to Tucker," Maddie said.

Finn made a move to leave, but I laid a hand on his arm.

"Listen, have you been in touch with Kristen's family?"

She shook her head. "I don't know where they are. She told people she was from Galveston, which pretty much guarantees that's the one place she's never been. I wouldn't know how to begin to find her people."

"Someone ought to," I said. "I know she had a past."

"That's an understatement," Maddie quipped. But there was no judgment in her voice, just a trace of sadness.

"Even so, somewhere there's someone who should know she's gone. A mother, a sister, maybe just a third-grade teacher who remembers a cute little gap-toothed blond girl. But somewhere, someone ought to mourn the girl she used to be."

# *chapter 22*

•

The main facility of the One Word Bible Church
was out FM411 a ways, just outside the Dalliance
city limits, where land was both cheap and plentiful.
Which was good, because the One Word Bible Church
was more a compound than a church. They boasted
a massive sanctuary that held thousands of the faithful every Sunday; a private elementary school with
two classrooms per grade; and a residential center that
housed visiting religious leaders as well as special
prayer retreats for the various study groups within the
church.

Tucker Gentry, though, kept his office in the Dalliance campus, where the youth group met. As we entered the building, located not far from the courthouse
square, I heard the sound of kids laughing and the
high-pitched wail of an electric guitar being tuned.

The whole place smelled like brownies. My stomach grumbled as we made our way down the linoleum-tiled hallway to Tucker's office.

One Word, as an organization, had a lot of money, but not much of it made its way to Tucker. When we tracked him down that morning, he was dressed in well-worn khakis and a simple oxford shirt. His hair was neatly combed, and a pair of glasses sat slightly askew on his face.

I knocked on the frame of his open office door.

"Hey, Tucker. Sorry to drop in unannounced."

"Tally! And, uh . . ."

"Finn Harper." Finn stepped forward and held out his hand. Tucker shook it. I'm guessing he was flying on autopilot at that point.

"I'm, uh . . ."

"Surprised?" I suggested.

His face twitched. "Yes, I guess that would sum it up. I don't get many visitors at all. Not many adults, at least. And, well, we, uh . . ."

Poor Tucker couldn't seem to figure out how to say what needed saying without being impolite. Thankfully for us both, I was past worrying much about "polite."

"Yeah, we don't exactly run in the same circles. Listen, can we sit?"

"Uh, sure. . . ." He stumbled to his feet as he belatedly realized that a lady had entered his orbit. He gestured to a pair of chairs upholstered in a nubby gray fabric. As he did so, I noticed the long, dark hairs dusting his fingers. They seemed out of place on his long, delicate, almost feminine hands.

We sat together, eyeing each other cautiously, before I got down to brass tacks.

"Who's suing you?" I asked.

"Excuse me?"

Finn took over. "Let's cut to the chase, here, Tucker. In case you're not aware, I'm a reporter for the *Dalliance News-Letter*." Apparently Tucker hadn't realized exactly who Finn was, because that tidbit of news washed what little color he had right away.

"I know you are being sued," Finn continued, "but I don't know why. And I'm curious. I could call in some favors, ask a bunch of questions, but I figure it might be in your best interest to tell us what's going on all on your own. Last thing you need is more gossip. Am I right?"

Tucker straightened in his seat. "I don't appreciate being strong-armed."

Finn and I had done this good-cop, bad-cop routine before. It was my turn.

"I totally understand, Tucker. We don't want to force your hand or pry into your private business. But Kristen Ver Steeg served papers on you and my cousin, Bree, on the very same day. And the next day Kristen was murdered. We're just trying to figure out what happened."

Tucker leaned back, as though he were trying to physically get away from me. "I wouldn't hurt anyone. Especially a woman."

"From what I've heard," Finn said, a hard edge to his words, "you prefer girls to women. So I'm not really sure what you're capable of."

Tucker leaped to his feet, genuine outrage stamped on his face. "If you dare to print Eloise Carberry's lies, I will sue you and your employer so fast—"

"Easy," I crooned. "No one is printing anything. Like I said, we're trying to set the record straight."

He eased back down in his desk chair, but his breathing came in short hitches. He was surely riled. "I do not have a thing for little girls. I am deeply in love with a wonderful Christian woman who has been working at an orphanage in Peru for two years. She's coming home next month, and I plan to propose."

He reached across his desk to a silver-framed photo and turned it around so we could see it. In the picture, Tucker stood side by side with a sweet-looking woman. She was his height with a soft, matronly figure—must have outweighed the scrawny preacher by thirty or forty pounds. Her pin-straight sandy hair draped over her shoulder, fanning over the bodice of her demure pink shirtdress, and falling all the way to her waist. There wasn't a lick of makeup on her face, but she glowed with a Madonna-like radiance, her eyes meeting the lens of the camera with clear, gentle kindness.

In the photo, Tucker's head was turned slightly, looking at the woman. The only word to describe his expression: adoration.

"That's me and Kim, last Christmas. In Peru. I was visiting."

"She's lovely," I said.

A smile flickered over his face. "Yes," he said simply.

Tucker couldn't be that good an actor. He loved his missionary woman as deeply as a man could love a woman. And I didn't think for an instant that the man who fell in love with Kim would also be attracted to teenyboppers. It just didn't make sense.

Which left me more confused than ever.

"Why would Eloise say such horrible things about you if they aren't true?"

"Eloise Carberry has a hole in her soul. I don't know where it came from, whether someone hurt her or if she was just born that way, but she's projecting her own sickness onto the world around her. She cannot fathom that I might have a love for her child that is Christ-like in its purity."

Wow. *Christ-like in its purity*? Was this guy for real? I exchanged a "what the heck?" glance with Finn.

"I know she looks like an ordinary woman," Tucker said, as though he'd read our thoughts. "But the devil takes many forms."

"Maybe you could be a little more specific," Finn suggested.

Tucker sighed. "Last spring, I chaperoned a trip to South Padre Island."

The infamous spring break trip Kyle had mentioned.

"Right," I said. "The tequila shooters."

Tucker winced. "Exactly. A bunch of the kids slipped out after curfew. Got horribly drunk. Made themselves sick."

"And you didn't report them," I said.

Tucker removed his glasses and rubbed the bridge of his nose. "That's true. In retrospect, I probably should have turned them in. But I didn't. That sort of over-indulgence reflects an injury to the spirit. Those kids needed ministry, not punishment. I invited them to join us at One Word, where they could find something other than liquor to make them happy."

"And did they take you up on that offer?" Finn asked.

"Only one of them. One soul, saved."

"Let me guess," I said. "Dani Carberry."

Tucker nodded. "She came to us, a lost lamb. And we offered her the peace of Christ. But her mother wanted to stand between her daughter and the true word of God. She forbade her child to pray with us."

"Is that why you didn't want her to chaperone that trip to Glen Rose?" I asked.

"Yes. What kind of Christian woman denies her child the opportunity to hear the true word of God? Eloise was not fit to care for her own child, let alone others. But Dani was made strong in the Lord, and she continued to seek our fellowship."

Uh-oh.

"So the Carberrys filed suit against me and the church. For interference with parental rights."

"Is that even a real thing?" I asked.

Finn answered. "Some states recognize a tort for in-terference with parental rights. It's usually used against a noncustodial parent. I have no idea about Texas."

Tucker snorted. "The church elders and I, we were anxious to vindicate our rights in court. I would have gone to the papers with news of Eloise Carberry's efforts to deny her child Christ's word on the very first day, but the Carberrys had the file sealed. Our attorneys said we couldn't discuss it."

I decided not to point out that Tucker wasn't very good at following his attorneys' instructions.

If he was telling the truth—and his righteous indignation suggested he was—then Tucker didn't have any motive to kill Kristen Ver Steeg. He didn't want to keep the lawsuit quiet or even make it go away. He wanted his day in court, his chance to defeat Satan with a gavel.

"If you were so gung ho to litigate, why did you leave that threatening message for Kristen?" Finn asked.

"What threatening message?"

"The one about minding her eternal soul."

Tucker smiled, without a trace of malice. "That wasn't a threat. Just good advice. The church and I, we didn't mind fighting evil because we recognized its true face. But it would be selfish to allow Miss Ver Steeg to take the side of Satan unwittingly, just so we could be vindicated. I gave her the information. She made the choice, of her own free will, to ignore it."

So. Tucker Gentry. Certifiable whack job, yes. Murderer, probably not. The man might do any number of crazy things in the name of his faith—I wouldn't even rule out the possibility of violence—but he would do it in the bright light of day. He saw himself as a champion of good. He wouldn't see any need to skulk around in the shadows. If he'd decided to gun down Kristen, he would have done it on the midway in broad daylight, not in the haunted rodeo.

Tucker's tale, though, presented another mystery. Why was Dani so determined to defy her mother and attend services at One Word? I knew that young converts were often the most zealous, but Dani didn't seem like the type of kid to get swept up by religious fervor. She was smart, well-to-do, from a stable home, and, most important, popular. As evidenced by her flag corps friends' willingness to cut off their hair in solidarity with her.

Maybe that was it. Maybe the cancer had made Dani go searching for meaning. And maybe there was something in the message at One Word that resonated with her in a way her own church's teachings didn't.

"Pastor Gentry, we blew a fuse on the big amp. Can I take the van to go buy a new one?"

I turned to face the newcomer with the blown fuse. His arms were sleeved in tattooes, including a blocky X on the back of each hand, and a silver stud in the shape of a fish adorned his lower lip. And the sides of his head were shaved in a modified Mohawk.

It was the hair that gave him away. He was the boy I'd seen groping Dani at the fair.

Tucker dug in his pants pocket and produced a set of keys. He held them up, jingling them, offering them to the boy. "Here you go, Matt," he said as the boy took them from his hand.

And there was my answer.

Kyle's friend Matt had a girlfriend all right. But her identity was a secret no longer. Dani's fervent devotion to the One Word Bible Church had less to do with love of God and more to do with love of her straight-edge beau . . . who wasn't even faithful to her.

# *chapter 23*

Finn and I regrouped at the A-la-mode.

"I feel like we're spinning our wheels," I said.

"Not true. We're crossing off suspects. That's helpful." He held up his right hand and began ticking off items on his fingers. "It probably wasn't Neck. And it probably wasn't Maddie. And it probably wasn't Tucker."

I still had my doubts about Maddie, but I decided to let that slide for the moment.

"Who's left?"

"I don't know." He took a sip of his soda. Diet. He'd put on a few pounds once we started dating. Apparently, between his own fabulous baking skills and my ice cream, he was finding it more and more difficult to keep his girlish figure.

"The one piece of information we're still missing, which I really, really wish we had, is that ethics question. We know it's out there, but all our attempts to guess what it might be about have failed to play."

"Hmm. Maybe she knew that Sonny was a fraud and wanted to go to the authorities. If Sonny knew his own lawyer was going to rat him out, maybe he killed her to protect his con."

Finn's eyes narrowed. "Maybe. But as much as I'd like to have some reason to pin this on Sonny, all we can do is speculate until we get our hands on that letter to the ethics board."

I nodded and sipped my own diet soda. "I could try Jason again. I feel bad. Poor kid is trying to do the right thing, you know."

Finn shook his head. "I think you're better off hitting up Maddie again. She may be turning over a new ethical leaf, but we have a bit of leverage against her. And she seemed sincere about wanting to know who killed Kristen."

"Oy," I moaned.

"Here, let me try." He fished his cell phone out of his pocket and dialed.

"Hey, Maddie. Finn Harper." A lopsided grin spread across his face. He covered the mouthpiece of the phone. "Maddie can cuss a blue streak," he said to me.

"Listen, we don't want to jam you up. Honest. I think we ought to swing by your office again and give you back that envelope so you can return it to your associate."

He paused, listening.

"You're a smart woman. But we wouldn't be so

crass as to resort to extortion. However, if a certain letter to an ethics board happened to be on the receptionist desk, it would let us know where we ought to file the envelope. Make sense?"

He flipped the phone closed, and held out his hand for the infamous envelope.

"Finn, I don't know about this. I mean, I want to get my hands on that ethics letter, too, but what Maddie's been doing is really bad. Selling out her clients to protect a bunch of drug dealers? I don't think I can help her cover that up."

"Oh, never fear," he said. "The envelope you got from Neck helped us figure out what Maddie was up to, but it's not really evidence of anything. She may feel more secure having it back in her hands, but I guarantee she won't be so pleased with me when she reads the article I'm planning to write."

"Yeah?"

He laughed. "Even if I didn't share your moral concerns with her behavior, I couldn't let an opportunity for a juicy story pass me by. I took notes at the courthouse, have a long list of clients of Maddie Jackson who are serving the max for their petty possession charges. I'm guessing that some of those guys who are cooling their heels in jail will be happy to talk to me about the advice Maddie gave them and how they chose her as their lawyer, especially once I tell them what she's been doing."

"You're my hero," I teased.

His smile faltered, and suddenly the moment felt

serious. He looked at me hard, as if he were trying to figure out a puzzle he saw in my eyes. Then he cleared his throat, and his smile returned . . . a bit forced.

"All I need is a cape. You sit tight, and I'll take care of this. Be right back."

After he left, I went back behind the counter and tidied up. I usually kept the place spotless, terrified of an impromptu health inspection. But that afternoon, the counter was littered with dirty scoops and drips of ice cream. What with splitting our crew between the store and the fair, me being busy investigating a murder, and Bree busy getting arrested, we'd been stretched a little thin.

"Finn leave?" Bree emerged from the back of the store, using her apron to dry her hands.

She'd been nervous around Finn ever since it came out that Alice was his daughter. I guess she'd been able to shove their one-night stand into a corner of her brain, pretend it had never happened, and she'd been able to laugh and joke and be normal around him. But she couldn't ignore it anymore. Alice was a living, breathing reminder.

"Yeah, but he'll be right back."

She leaned back against the counter, lifting each leg in turn to flex her ankles. She insisted on wearing heels when she worked, and by the end of the day her calves were always aching.

"Are we okay?" she asked.

I wiped up a smear of butter pecan. "We're okay."

When she exhaled, I realized she'd been holding her breath.

"Dang, Bree, you and I have been through everything together. I've been there for every one of your marriages and every one of your divorces. You helped me take care of my mom, and held me when she died. You were there to kick me in the pants when my marriage to Wayne ended, kept me from slipping into a horrible wallow of self-pity. At this point, I don't think there's anything on God's green earth you could do to break us apart."

She nudged my leg with the toe of one strappy, high-heeled sandal. "What about you two?"

I didn't have to ask who she meant. "I don't know."

"Tally, I couldn't stand it if what I did came between you and Finn. You two, you were meant to be. For crying out loud, he came back after seventeen years. Seventeen years, and still you've got that magic between you. Don't let that go."

I looked at her then. Saw the pain and pleading in her face. "Honey, I just don't know yet. But I'll tell you this. If things don't work out between me and Finn, it's not on you. Not one little bit. It's on him, for leaving Dalliance all those years ago. It's on me, for pushing him away in the first place. But it's not on you."

A tear slipped down her cheek, and she pulled me close in a fierce hug.

"Ahem."

Bree and I pulled apart when Finn cleared his throat.

He stood there, a few feet away, looking at as both. He knew we'd reached some sort of peace. And I could see the question in his eyes, whether that peace included him.

"Sorry to interrupt," he said, "but you two are gonna want to hear this." He held up a stapled packet of papers. "It's quite a story."

The Carberrys lived in the same moneyed neighborhood where Finn had grown up and to which he had returned to take care of his mother. Two-story brick houses squatted on generous squares of too-green lawn, each suburban fiefdom separated from the others by stands of bamboo and hedges of holly. The children in this neighborhood splashed away the summers in backyard pools, the primal scents of beef and charcoal adding a certain urgency to their late-evening games of capture-the-flag.

Mike Carberry opened the door to Finn's knock. He was in his midforties, had been just a year behind my ex-husband, Wayne, in school. Mike had grown up a few blocks over, left Dalliance to earn a degree in kinesiology at Oklahoma State before returning home to find a job. He'd stumbled into a position at the *Dalliance News-Letter*, but ended up being a decent reporter. He didn't have a particular gift with words, but folks in Dalliance trusted him. That trust opened doors, and access mattered more than eloquence in small-town journalism.

We'd caught him on a day off. He wore paint-stained cargo shorts, a Dalliance High Wild-Catters T-shirt, athletic socks, and a pair of orange molded-plastic clogs.

"Hey, guys," he said. "Didn't expect you two. Come on in."

He held the door wide. As we passed him, he yawned

hugely, opening his mouth wide enough that I could see the gold crowns on his molars. At the apex of the yawn, he reached back to grab a handful of his own mussed brown hair as though he were trying to hold his head on his shoulders.

"Sorry," he muttered. "I was napping."

I smiled. "I know the feeling. It's been a crazy couple of days."

"Ain't that the truth? Can I get y'all something to drink?"

"No, thanks, Mike. Look, we were wondering if Eloise was at home. Maybe we could talk to you both for a few minutes."

Something in Finn's tone must have signaled that we hadn't just stopped by to hang out. Mike stood up a little straighter, a little more alert.

"Sure. Eloise is out back, working in the garden."

Mike led the way through their tasteful house. With walls and floors covered in tones of coffee—from a rich mocha to a pale café au lait, furniture upholstered in traditional blues and dark greens, and absolutely no clutter, the house felt like a model home. I glanced at Mike's rumpled clothes and wondered where his den was, the man cave where he was allowed to put his feet on the couch and eat in front of the TV.

As we passed through the great room at the back of the house, I noticed a family portrait hanging over the mantel: Mike's thinning hair combed neatly over his bald spot, Dani with her natural, caramel locks in a glossy bob, the whole family wearing matching red sweaters and khaki pants.

In the picture, there was a look in Eloise's eyes, a look that mingled triumph and challenge. As if sitting for that portrait was the equivalent of her planting her flag at the summit of Everest . . . and she was daring the world to try to knock her off.

We slipped from the cool dim of the house through the sliding door in the back and into a perfect suburban retreat. The motor for the pool filters hummed softly, and in the distance I could hear children playing a rambunctious game of Marco Polo.

Eloise knelt with her back to us, a blue latex pad protecting her knees from the pebbly aggregate of the pool's patio. She wore a broad-brimmed straw hat, though she worked in the shade, yanking weeds from between hostas that were spaced with military precision, as though the plants were afraid to grow too close together. I looked around at the raised beds that circled the pool deck. All of the plants were spaced apart from each other, lonely soldiers guarding the perimeter of the Carberry compound.

"Eloise," Mike called. "We have visitors."

"What?" Eloise twisted around, raising the back of her wrist to her forehead and squinting at us from beneath the floppy brim of her hat. "Oh, Finn! And Tally? Good heavens, Mike. You should have told me we were expecting company."

"Sorry, Eloise. We dropped by without calling."

A flash of irritation tightened her features, but then she smiled as she struggled to her feet.

"Our house is always open," she said. "What brings you by?"

"Maybe we should sit," Mike suggested, ushering us to a round, umbrella-topped patio table.

Finn held out an iron-backed chair for me. Mike tried to do the same for Eloise, but she brushed his hand away and seated herself.

"What's this all about?" Eloise bit out the question through teeth clenched in a hard smile.

"I, uh, heard that Dani is sick," I said.

For a heartbeat, Eloise studied me with narrowed eyes. "Yes," she said simply.

Finn cleared his throat. "Mike? You never said anything."

Mike's shoulders tensed, but he didn't say anything.

"Karla Faye down at the Hair Apparent said Dani's lost her hair to chemo," I continued. "She's wearing a wig now."

"That's right."

"There's a rumor going around that Kristen Ver Steeg was going to disqualify Dani from the pageant because of her wig. Which sounds pretty coldhearted."

Eloise sniffed, as though the mere mention of Kristen had offended her sensibilities.

"That's what Cookie told you the night before Kristen was murdered, right? That Kristen was going to kick Dani out of the competition?"

She looked over my shoulder, studying her own neat and soulless backyard. "So?"

"So, Cookie was wrong," Finn said.

Eloise's head snapped around. "What?"

"Cookie was wrong. Kristen didn't call for that meeting of the pageant judges because she wanted to disqualify Dani, or any other contestant. She was planning to recuse herself from the competition."

"I don't . . . ," Eloise stammered.

"It's true," I said. "At the ice cream competition the other day, Jackie Conway mentioned that Kristen had contacted her the day before she was murdered and asked Jackie to take over all her responsibilities at the fair, including the pageant. I didn't understand then why, and I was too distracted to ask, but now I know it was because of you."

"Me?" Eloise gasped.

"Well, you and Dani," I amended.

Finn leaned forward. "We know about your lawsuit against Tucker Gentry and the One Word Bible Church."

Mike piped up. "It wasn't right, what that preacher did. He had no business interfering with how we raise our child, especially when it comes to something as important as our faith."

"You're right," I said. "Tucker overstepped his bounds. But that doesn't excuse what you did."

The sliding glass door whooshed open and Dani bounded out onto the patio. "Mom? I want to go . . . Oh. Hey, Mr. Harper." She glanced at me, puzzled.

"Hi, Dani," Finn said. "You look like you're feeling good."

Dani's face turned crimson beneath the bangs of her espresso-colored wig. She wore tiny denim shorts, a tight Texas Rangers ring tee, and flip-flops. Chipped turquoise polish coated her finger- and toenails. She was the picture of the all-American girl.

"I am, Mr. Harper. Thanks." Her mouth tightened, and she slid a hard glare toward her mother.

"Dani's been doing much better. It's a miracle, really," Eloise said, a tremor in her voice.

"Aw, come on, Eloise," Finn said. "Let's cut it out, okay? We know it's not a miracle. We know Dani is perfectly fine. Always has been."

"What?" Eloise gasped, drawing herself rigid with outrage. "How dare you come into our house and—"

"Mom! Enough. Jeez, they know, okay?"

Mike slumped in his chair, as if he wanted to slither under the table and just trickle away. Eloise looked back and forth, from me and Finn to her daughter.

The silence stretched out to uncomfortable lengths, while Eloise tried to figure out her next move. Finally, Dani made it for her.

With a sigh, she pulled off the wig and plucked off the skullcap she wore beneath it. She sighed again, this time in relief, as she ruffled her fingers through the short, purple hair she had liberated.

"That thing is so freakin' hot," she grumbled.

In an instant, she transformed from all-American girl to the goth girl I'd seen canoodling with young Matt the night of the karaoke contest. Matt was cheating on Dani with Dani, two sides of the very same girl.

The difference between Dani with the wig and Dani without was staggering. My brain understood what had happened, but my eyes were still trying to figure out how one girl could disappear and leave someone else in her place. Her hair changed, but more than that: the expression on her face, the angles of her body, everything. With the wig gone and her spiky purple locks crowning her head like aster petals, her face softened, and her stance lowered, as though her center of gravity had dropped a few inches. She looked simultaneously more relaxed and more primitive. Less Disney Pocahontas, more tribal shaman.

"You weren't wearing the wig the night of the karaoke contest," I said.

"Dani!" Eloise gasped. "I told you you weren't to step foot outside this house without the wig."

Dani shrugged. She'd been busted, but clearly she didn't care. "You try living through this heat wave with two pounds of fake hair sitting on your head. I swear, you got the hottest, heaviest wig you could find just to spite me."

"Well, now you've ruined everything," Eloise said, even though Dani hadn't been caught during her wigless excursion. "I hope you're happy now."

"I am. I told you this was stupid, Mom. We couldn't keep pretending I was sick forever."

"Show your mother some respect," Mike said, but he was just going through the motions. He'd clearly checked out emotionally.

"She didn't show me any respect," Dani said. "She'd rather people think I have cancer than let them know who I really am."

Eloise laughed. "Who you really are? Please. You're seventeen. You don't have a clue who you really are. And you're certainly not some purple-haired punk."

Dani pointed to her own head. "I *do* have purple

hair, Mom. It's just hair. Spiky and purple or long and brunette, it's just hair. It's not who I am. You're the only one who thinks my hair matters."

"I'm not the only one," Eloise insisted. "The pageant—"

"I told you, I don't even want to do that stupid pageant. Bunch of vain girls trotting around like their outsides are so important. That's your thing, Mom, not mine. It matters to *you*. The only thing that matters to me is Matt."

"Enough!" Eloise spat. "Go to your room."

Dani shot her mother a "get real" look, but turned on her heel and slammed into the house. Whether she went to her room or straight out the front door and off into the unknown, I had no idea. But we were back to just the adults on the patio.

"How did you know?" Eloise asked.

"Kristen," Finn said.

Kristen's letter to the ethics board provided every horrible and absurd detail. Seems Dani's passion for Matt, the über-Christian straight-edge musician, had prompted her to shave off half her hair and dye what was left a brilliant purple. In addition to being a general embarrassment for the prim and proper Eloise, the "artifice" would disqualify Dani from the Lantana Round-Up Rodeo Queen Pageant in which she was already entered.

Apparently Eloise came up with a solution. No one would even know her child had desecrated her hair. She simply got Dani a wig. But even the best wig would be sussed out by the pageant police . . . so she also concocted a story about Dani having cancer, losing her hair to chemo.

The ruse didn't really hurt anyone . . . unless you counted the flag corps girls who cropped their own hair in solidarity.

But as the Carberrys' attorney, Kristen knew Dani had cut her hair, that she wasn't sick. And that put Kristen in a tricky situation. First, she wasn't sure whether faking cancer constituted child abuse that she, as an officer of the court, was obligated to report. And, second, she didn't know how to square her role as pageant director—which she did, indeed, take very seriously, despite the fact that she wasn't really a veteran of the pageant circuit—with her ethical obligation of privilege to her clients.

"The ethics board informed Kristen that you weren't breaking any law," Finn said, "so she had no basis for breaking privilege. They recommended that, if she felt conflicted about her role as pageant director, she should step down. That's what she planned to do."

"That's why she recused herself from the dispute between you and Tucker over his ice cream, because she had every intention of stepping down from her position as judge entirely. She was turning over both jobs to Jackie Conway so she wouldn't be torn up about keeping your secret."

"I didn't know," Eloise said.

Finn shook his head. "No, no, you didn't. You thought Kristen was going to break privilege and tell everyone about your lie. What I can't figure out is how you thought you could keep Dani's condition a secret. Eventually, it would come out in the litigation . . . that was part of your case, that Tucker had pulled Dani into this crowd of kids who were having a bad influence on her."

"I . . . I didn't think."

"No," I said. "No, you didn't."

"So, let me get this straight," Cal said. "Dani Carberry doesn't have cancer."

"Nope. Just a stupid haircut."

"And you think maybe Eloise was so torqued up about this pageant thing that she actually killed Kristen?" Cal didn't look convinced.

The four of us—Bree, Finn, Cal, and I—were gathered around a table at the A-la-mode. Beth lurked behind the counter, pretending not to eavesdrop.

"I don't know for sure," I said, "but I know Bree didn't do it, and Eloise had at least as much motive as Bree. Plus, like I've been saying, Eloise was a gymnast. She could have hoisted herself up onto that balcony. You yourself said the shooter could have been up there."

"*Could* have, Tally. Maybe." He shook his head. "I'm just not seein' it."

"Just talk to her, Cal. Bree deserves to have you investigate every possible alternative."

Cal's eyes slid to my cousin and then away again. He cleared his throat. "Yeah, I'll talk to Eloise."

Dang, I was starting to think that Cal had a crush on Bree. And by the way she was blushing, red as her hair, it might be mutual.

"I'm not promising anything here, but I'll talk to her," he repeated as he got to his feet.

"Oh, I almost forgot." He patted his pockets, pulled out a cell phone, and held it up. "Alice's phone. We found it in the center console of Kristen's car."

"Don't you need that for evidence or something? I mean, it backs up Bree's story," Finn said.

"We duped the SIM card, we verified that Kristen's prints were on it, took pictures of it in the console. We've got what we need. And it helps Bree, but it doesn't get her off the hook. We still don't know whether Kristen or Alice used the phone to call Bree that night. And even if Kristen arranged the meeting. . . ."

Cal was right, of course. The phone verified part of Bree's story, but it didn't clear up what had happened inside the haunted rodeo. Still, it was good news.

Bree took the phone from Cal, and, sure enough, his fingers lingered just a touch too long before he let go.

"So?" Finn asked as the door swung shut behind Cal. "Do you think he'll get anywhere?"

I shrugged. "I'm not sure. But I think he's motivated to try."

"Huh." Bree was monkeying with Alice's phone. "Here's that picture of Sonny Alice was talking about. He was pretty handsome, wasn't he?"

She handed me the phone. The picture was grainy, having been scanned from an old Polaroid, but it showed Sonny, hair combed in a black pompadour, holding Alice. A nimbus of wispy strawberry hair stuck out from her tiny head, and her head was tipped back as she laughed, tiny teeth bared in glee. Sonny watched Alice, the smile on his own face more reserved but still radiant.

He might have bailed on them, but he obviously loved his child.

I hit the NEXT button on the phone and revealed a picture Alice must have taken from the Dutch Oven parking lot, while she was sitting on the Bonnie's hood waiting for Sonny. Even though she'd shot the picture through a plate-glass window, it was clearer than the old picture. In the new one, Sonny had his back to the camera. The two women sitting with him, though, were facing the window, one on either side of him.

Kristen, in fact, was staring right out the window, looking directly into the camera. Alice must have snapped the picture at the exact moment Kristen noticed her outside.

I flipped back and forth between the two photos for a second. Had Kristen ever tipped her head back and laughed the way Alice did in that picture? Had her daddy held her and studied her face with the loving awe I saw in Sonny's eyes? Who missed Kristen?

"Bree? Can you watch the store this afternoon?"

"Sure, honey. Why?"

"I'm gonna take a drive."

# *chapter 24*

Under normal circumstances, I wouldn't be caught dead walking into a dark, windowless establishment called the Pony Up Gentlemen's Club. But looking at that picture of Alice with Sonny, and thinking of all the years Finn had missed with her, made me want to find Kristen's family. As I'd said to Maddie, someone out there would mourn her, and she deserved that connection with her kin.

Walking into a strip club seemed a small price to pay for the possibility of finding someone who knew where Kristen had come from. It wasn't much of a lead, but her Miss Am-Cam bio had a link to the Pony Up Gentlemen's Club. I could only hope that Kristen had worked there long enough to make an impression on someone who happened to still be around.

The inside of the Pony Up had the same utilitarian

anonymity as the outside: dinged lino tiles on the floor, featureless round wooden tables, a Formica-topped bar, everything in shades of brown and tan. To my surprise, the club had customers, even though it wasn't yet suppertime. A young couple—him in jeans and a ball cap, her in a short skirt and a tank top—shot pool at the table near the front door.

Deeper in the room, a couple of men sat at the bar-height runway where the dancers did their thing. As I made my way toward the bar, I studied one of the guys. He wore a denim vest over a plaid shirt, his pants the most colorless color I've ever seen. He cradled a coffee mug between his gnarled hands, and he seemed far more interested in its contents than in the skinny young woman grinding her privates not two feet from his face.

The tableau struck me as excruciatingly sad.

I turned to the bartender, and found her studying me through a haze of cigarette smoke. A mountain of platinum hair dwarfed her deeply lined face. A red-sequined tank top showed a generous amount of age-spotted décolletage.

"Hey," I said, taking a seat on one of the padded stools.

"You lost?" she asked, red lips peeling back in a smile. Her teeth were tiny and spaced far apart, as if maybe she'd never lost her milk teeth. The juxtaposition of the old harlot's face and the child's teeth gave me the shivers.

"I don't think so," I said. "Could I get a soda? Diet."

"Sure, hon." She dipped a clear plastic cup in the

ice bin and filled it with the soda gun. She tossed a cocktail napkin on the bar and set my drink on top.

She didn't ask for money, but I laid a five on the bar.

"I'm actually looking for some information," I said.

She took a deep drag on her cigarette and blew the smoke in a tight stream, straight toward the ceiling. "Are you a private eye? You don't look like a cop."

"None of the above. This woman I know, she died. I'm trying to find her family to let them know, but she was pretty quiet about her early years. She used to work here, though."

"How long ago? I been here, dancing and tending bar, for about twenty years, but if it's longer than that, you'd have to ask the owner. He doesn't come in until nine or ten."

"She was a dancer here in the mid-1990s." I pulled Alice's phone out, found the picture of Kristen, Sonny, and Char. "This woman here," I said, pointing to Kristen. "Sorry the picture's so small."

The bartender leaned over to look at the screen, squinting at it. "Well, I'll be. That's Kiki. She looks real good." She laughed. "Kiki said she was going to go to law school."

"She did. She was a lawyer."

"Son of a . . . but you said she's dead?"

I nodded.

"Well, that's too bad. Poor kid. Did she die easy?"

I didn't figure there was much point in lying to her. "No. Afraid not."

She clicked her tongue against her teeth. "Poor kid. I'm not sure I can be much help. I remember Kiki talking about being in foster care. Her daddy ran out on her and her mama when she was little, Mama couldn't make ends meet. But that's about it. Sad story. Hear it every day around here."

"She never said where she was from?"

She shook her head. "No. Someplace east, I think. Got that impression, anyway.

"She was a real good dancer. Better than any of these girls."

She gestured toward the stage, and my eyes followed the movement. The dancer had given up on the old man and his coffee, and now she was working the pole. Her dance steps led her away from the actual pole, and then she pivoted, took a gazellelike leap toward the pole, grabbed it with both hands, and—in a move I couldn't entirely follow—swung up so her feet were above her head. My jaw dropped as she curled her upper body up, essentially climbing the pole with arms and legs.

"Better than that?" I asked.

The bartender laughed, a sound like a rusty hinge. "Way better than that. But not as good as Shirley."

I turned back to the old woman. "Who?"

"Shirley. This girl." She tapped Alice's phone, which I still held in my hand.

I was so intent on Alice's phone that I almost didn't hear my own ringing from the depths of my purse. I set Alice's phone on the bar, fished out my own, and saw that the call was from Bree. I raised a finger in apology to the bartender and flipped my phone open to take the call.

"Eloise has an alibi," Bree announced without pre-amble. "She was at a freakin' League of Methodist La-dies meeting, so she's got a dozen of Dalliance's most upstanding citizens ready to swear she was in a house of God when Kristen was killed."

Well, that bit the big one.

Bree started to say something else, but the bartender staring hard at Alice's phone distracted me.

"Bree, can you hold on a second?" I said into the phone. I covered the mouthpiece with my hand. "What's wrong?" I asked the bartender.

"What? Oh, nothing. I just can't believe how good she looks. Almost didn't recognize her, but I'm pretty sure that's her. Shirley could have worked the clubs in Dallas, maybe even gone to Vegas, but she got herself a little drug habit. Did her in right quick."

"Shirley?" I repeated, totally lost.

"Yeah, Shirley." The bartender tapped Alice's phone again. "Surprised she couldn't tell you about Kiki's peo-ple. They were real close back when they both danced here."

I looked at the phone on the bar, the picture of Kris-ten, Sonny, and Char. "This woman?" I asked, pointing to Char. "Her name is Shirley?"

By then, the bartender was looking at me like I had a screw loose. "Yeah."

"And she was a stripper here?"

"Yeah. Until Joe fired her for the drugs. I would have thought she'd be dead by now. Most of the users don't make it long. But she looks real good, too."

I stared at the picture. Char had been a stripper. Of

course. Sonny had said that Char hired Kristen, that she knew her from the old days. Somehow, the two dancers must have kept in touch over the years.

I let my gaze drift back to the stage, where the dancer was now swinging around the pole in a dizzying spiral.

A pole. Really nothing more than a pipe anchored between floor and ceiling.

A lot like the pipe that braced the saloon facade in the haunted rodeo attraction. Heck, from where I was sitting, it looked as if the pole was about the same size as that pipe.

I looked back at the picture on the tiny screen of Alice's phone. And I wondered if Char—Shirley—could still work a pole the way she used to.

I let my hand fall away from the mouthpiece of my own phone. "Bree? You still there?"

"Where else would I be?" she snapped. "I can't believe the thing with Eloise didn't pan out. Now we're back to square one."

"Maybe not. I think I may know who did it. Though I'm still not one hundred percent sure why."

"Spill it."

"I think it might have been Sonny's friend Char."

"Crap! Really? Why?"

"I'll explain it all when I get back to the A-la-mode."

# *chapter 25*

I had just pulled off the interstate when my phone rang again. I was at a light, so I answered.

"They're leaving," Bree said. She sounded panicked.

"Who?"

"Sonny and Char. Finn just stopped by to say that he'd seen Sonny at the Parlay Inn. Sonny said he and Char were hitting the road tonight. Finn thought maybe I should break the news to Sonny about Alice before he left."

"Why are they leaving so suddenly?"

"Sonny gave Finn some story about a family emergency, but Finn heard a rumor that one of their potential investors did a little poking around and might have called the feds."

"Whoa."

"If Char did it," Bree said, "we have to stall them."

"Where are they staying?"

"At the Ramada by the interstate."

I looked to my left. There was the giant red Ramada Inn sign.

"I'm right there. I'll stall. You call Cal and tell him to hightail it over here."

"Like the man would do my bidding." I thought I detected a tiny note of hope in her voice, as if maybe she wanted me to tell her that Cal would jump through hoops of fire if she asked him to.

"I think he might be inclined to help you out, Bree. But if he balks, make up an excuse. Anything to get him to the Ramada before Sonny and Char hit the road."

I'm sure she was violating company policy, but the woman at the front desk recognized me from the A-la-mode and handed over Sonny and Char's room number with a smile.

I knocked on the door to room 307.

"Jesus, Sonny, did you forget your key a—"

The door swung open, and Char stopped midsentence when she saw me. She was dressed to travel in low-slung jeans and a baby-doll T-shirt, her paprika-colored hair in a ponytail high on her head. I hadn't noticed before that she was so much younger than Sonny.

"Hey, Char."

"Sonny isn't here."

"Oh. Shoot. Well, mind if I wait for him? It's really important."

She narrowed her eyes. I could almost see her weighing the pros and cons in her head, trying to decide which was better: getting rid of me or figuring out why I was there.

Finally, she stepped back and let the door swing open. "Suit yourself."

They'd pulled the drapes in the room, so the only light came from a couple of brass lamps. I made my way to the upholstered chair by the window and sat. Char flipped closed the suitcase sitting on the king-sized bed and zipped it before stepping over to the vanity.

"You leaving?" I asked innocently.

"Just for a few days. Family emergency."

"Oh. Sorry to hear that."

Char reached up to wrap her ponytail into a loose bun. As she did so, her skimpy T-shirt rode up her torso, and I caught a glimpse of green on her abdomen. An arc of dark green . . . a flash of gold . . . a tattoo of a champagne bottle.

I gasped. "Spumanti?"

Charlize slid her eyes to the side to meet my gaze in the mirror. For a second, I thought she would protest, but then her lips curled in a feline smile. "At one time," she conceded. "Shirley, Spumanti, Charlene, Shireen—" She punctuated each name by stabbing another pin in her hair. Her arms dropped to her sides. "Just names."

"You look . . . different."

She rolled her shoulders in a graceful shrug. "Better living through chemistry? A little silicone here, some collagen there, enzyme peels, bleach for my teeth, colored contacts." She shrugged again, and flopped back to sit on the bed. "And Pilates. Lots of Pilates."

"I can't believe . . ."

"Lordy, Tally. Can't finish a sentence, can you?" She laughed, a low and knowing sound. "Can't believe what? That Sonny and I are still together?"

Bingo.

"I—uh, no, of course not."

"Oh, it's okay. I know what y'all thought of me. Just a sad little junkie looking for a father figure, right? Figured Sonny'd dump me for a new flavor-of-the-month the way he dumped Bree?" She narrowed her too-blue eyes. "I *was* a sad little junkie. But I was also a smart little junkie. You know my secret to holding on to Sonny?"

I shook my head.

"Sonny likes new things, right? So I became some-one new every chance I got. Hell's bells, Sonny has moved from one girl to the next . . . but every one of them has been me."

A smart little junkie, indeed.

"I got good at reading his moods, paid attention to the girls he watched with that special look in his eyes. Got a boob job after I caught him panting after this double-E cup in Cincinnati. Went red when he said Reba McEntire was foxy. Made myself into his dream girl."

A tiny crease marred the space between her eyes, and the corners of her plump, glossy lips tightened. "For some reason, I never noticed that his dream girl—

the girl I see in the mirror every morning—looks just like Bree."

"But Sonny left Bree," I said. "He chose you."

Charlize or Shirley or whatever her name was rolled her eyes and blew out an exasperated breath. "In case you didn't notice, Sonny's an idiot. He ran off because he got an itch in his drawers. And he didn't choose me. I just happened to be the nearest warm body when that itch came over him."

"The result's the same," I insisted.

"No, it's not. Sonny would have come back to Dalliance with his tail between his legs within a week of leaving, 'cept he was sure Bree would geld him with a kitchen knife.

"I guess I was an okay substitute. But Bree's got one thing I can't get from a cosmetic counter or a plastic surgeon."

"What?"

"Alice."

"Oh."

"I could maybe compete with Sonny's ex, but I can't hold a candle to his little girl. He loves that child."

"He's got a funny way of showing it. He denied her the minute he got to town."

Char snagged a short black leather jacket from the head of the bed and shrugged into it. "You're so naive, Tally. That lawsuit wasn't Sonny's idea. It was mine."

"But he went along with it. He must not have cared that much about Alice."

"It didn't really have anything to do with Alice.

Look, the con . . ." She tilted her head in an inquiring angle. "You know it's all a con, right?"

I nodded.

"Good. It's exhausting, you know? Anyway, the con required Sonny to flash around a lot of cash. But that meant Bree would probably go after Sonny for child support, and that would mean Bree, the county, and God knows who else poking around in Sonny's financial records. It wouldn't take long for them to figure out there was no fortune. We've been living from scam to scam for fifteen years. At the moment, we don't have nothing but a lease on that fancy car and the clothes on our backs. We'll be lucky to get out of town before the hotel realizes our credit cards are no good and call the law on us.

"We had to stall. I came up with the idea of claiming Sonny wasn't the daddy. We figured there'd be a week or two before we got to court, then another couple of weeks for the DNA results . . . by then, we'd be long gone."

"Sounds like a good plan."

"It was," she huffed. "But then Sonny got drunk and spilled the beans to Kristen, and she started whining about how she was an officer of the court and couldn't—what did she say?" She screwed up her face in concentration. "Oh, right, she couldn't perpetrate a fraud. It would be an abuse of process. Blah, blah, blah. All a bunch of lawyer talk for 'I'm gonna sell you guys down the river.'"

"So Kristen really did ask to meet Bree that morning?"

"Yeah. Can you believe that? I watch enough TV to know that she wasn't supposed to do that. We had privilege."

I had a sneaking suspicion Char was right. Kristen might have had an ethical obligation to withdraw from the case, to not help Sonny and Char, but she probably wasn't supposed to have a private tête-à-tête with Bree, either.

"She was full of shit, too. Kristen didn't have any problem with fraud. Her whole life was a fraud. She walked around this town all high-and-mighty in her fancy shoes with her law degree, but she got started just like me. Working a pole to buy meth. Heck, she was worse than me. Even I didn't do porn."

I filed away that little tidbit for future reference: on the sleaziness scale, apparently "stripping" and "snorting crank" were above "porn."

"She knew we were scamming the minute we got to town. Like I said, she and I went way back. She knew I wasn't born to the name Charlize Guidry, and I sure as heck wasn't in the oil business. She didn't seem to have any problem with taking a cut of our money until that night."

"That night? What night?"

"The night before she died. We met Kristen at the Dutch Oven, late, to talk about the incorporation papers for the fracking scam. We'd copied some boilerplate language from a form contract we found on the Internet, but we wanted to make sure we had the heading right for the Texas courts. We didn't want to involve Kristen too much in that side of our plan, but we wanted to make sure our i's were dotted and our t's were crossed.

"Sonny'd already had a six-pack, maybe more, and then he ordered shots with his pancakes. Pretty soon he was all weepy and gabbing away. At first, Kristen just sat there and listened." Char laughed. "We'd both spent plenty of hours listening to drunk guys babble. It's an art. Her eyes were all unfocused, staring out the front window of the restaurant, and every now and then she'd nod. Just like you'd do if you were listening to a john talk about how much he really loves his wife but she just doesn't get him anymore."

She sobered again. "Then, all of a sudden, she said she wanted to get her smokes from the car. She was gone for maybe five minutes, then came back and didn't even have her cigs."

That must have been when she saw Alice sitting on the hood of the Bonnie outside and gone out to talk to her.

"After that," Char continued, "it was like she'd blown a gasket. She chews out Sonny about how she wasn't gonna have any part in his scam. Worked herself into a tizzy and then finally excused herself to use the ladies'. I followed her, real quiet. I heard her in the stall, talking to Bree."

*Using Alice's phone,* I thought, *which had Bree's land-line number programmed into the contact list.*

"I knew she was going to tell."

"Why would she call Bree? Why not call the cops?"

"Like I said, she didn't really care about our con. At least, not enough to risk her license by going public with privileged information." Char shook her head. "No, she blew up about the fracking scam, but I know Kristen—it was the paternity suit that bothered her. And, besides, it was safer to spill the beans to Bree than to go to the authorities. Less chance of her getting in trouble with the bar."

Again, I guessed Char had hit the nail on the head. Given Kristen's own experience with a deadbeat dad, I bet Kristen identified with both Bree and Alice. And, from what Jason and Maddie had said, Kristen had a hard time reconciling the ethical obligations of her profession with her own sense of morality.

"Why did you have to kill her?" I asked. "Why not just pack up and leave, hit the road and try your con in some other town?"

Char cocked her head, puzzled. "Oh no. I didn't plan to kill Kristen. I planned to kill Bree."

# chapter 26

It felt as if all the blood drained from my body, leaving behind nothing but aching cold.

"Bree?"

"Yeah. Stupid contacts. They're expensive. I had to choose between colored lenses and ones that correct my astigmatism. Duh, I went with the blue contacts. Color's called Marine Magic. But I can't see for crap in the dark. First bullet, I think I took out a power line, and I only had time to get off one more shot before I heard people coming."

I couldn't believe how close Bree had come to dying. Saved by this crazy woman's own vanity.

Char got up again, returned to the dressing table, and bent down to study herself in the mirror. She brushed her finger along her jawline, testing the elasticity of that delicate skin. "At first I thought, 'Oh well.

I need Bree gone. Prison's as good as dead, right?' But then Sonny started talking about how Alice was gonna need her daddy. Talk about jumping out of the frying pan and into the fire. Sonny getting all paternal was the last thing I wanted."

She sighed. "The way I saw it, after I screwed up trying to kill Bree and she got in trouble with the law, there were two ways this could play out. Either we stuck around and Sonny decided it's time to be a father . . . in which case he would definitely kill the con and probably dump me. Or else I convinced him it's time to bail. So I told him the FBI was on to us."

Wow. Really smart junkie.

There was a knock at the door. Cal. Finally.

But when Char peeped through the peephole—a prudent step she hadn't taken when I knocked—she laughed. "Well, it's turning into a regular hen party."

She swung open the door, and there—of course— was Bree. How could my cousin miss an opportunity to stumble into trouble?

"Come on in, shug," Char gushed.

"Hey, Char. Tally." Bree managed to keep a smile on her face, but as she looked from Char's big smile to my look of misery, I saw the realization in her eyes . . . the realization that this was not a good scene.

Char shut the door behind Bree and threw the safety latch. She stood there, between me and Bree and freedom.

"What's up?" Bree asked.

Char looked over her to catch my gaze. "I take it she's not quite up to speed."

I shook my head.

Char sighed. "Too bad. Well, the short version is that you two picked the wrong time to stop by. Another hour, and Sonny and I would have been gone. But now I've gotta think on my feet."

She reached into the pocket of her leather jacket and drew out a gun. Just a tiny thing, not much bigger than a deck of playing cards. But I knew that, when it came to firearms, size didn't matter nearly as much as aim and determination.

To her credit, Bree kept her cool. She took a step back, her legs hit the edge of the bed, and she sat down hard. But she didn't scream or cry or anything. Me, I was too scared to make a sound.

"I think I can make this work," Char mused. "Bree comes over with Tally and has a hissy fit about me and Sonny. Woman scorned stuff. Pulls out a gun. Tally's here to stop her, but a struggle ensues . . . Bree shoots Tally by accident, I shoot Bree in self-defense."

Bree shook her head. "Sorry, darlin'. I don't think that's going to fly."

"Why not?"

Before Char finished her question, the pounding commenced.

"Charlize Guidry? This is Cal McCormack from the Dalliance Police Department. I'm here to conduct a welfare check."

"That's why," Bree said softly.

"I'm fine," Char yelled through the door. "You can go."

"No, ma'am. I'm afraid I can't. We got a report of

suspicious activity in your room, and I need to verify with my own eyes that you're okay."

"Go. Away."

"No, ma'am."

Cal must have gotten a passkey from the manager, because the door opened as far as the safety latch would allow. Char jumped back as if she'd been stung.

Bree, always quick on her feet, took advantage of Char's momentary confusion to jump up and knock the gun from Char's hand.

Char dived for the gun, but by then I was in motion. I scrambled off the chair, kicked the gun under the bed, and sat on Char, while Bree lunged for the door.

"Ow!" Cal yelled as Bree slammed the door closed so she could release the safety latch.

Bree threw open the door. "She's got a gun," she yelled as she stepped out of Cal's way.

Cal pushed his way into the room, gun drawn, and froze when he saw me sitting on Char.

"Lord a'mighty, Tally," he swore softly. "This is the second time in six months I've busted into a room to find you sittin' on someone." He sighed. "We gotta get you a new hobby."

# chapter 27

Within twenty-four hours, everything changed. Char—nee Shirley Mackintee—had been hauled off to jail. Sonny had been arrested for fraud, but Cal said he was already talking about a deal: immunity in exchange for his testimony against Char and a return of all the fake investment money. He'd taken the news of Char's crimes pretty hard, but he'd taken the news that he wasn't Alice's daddy even harder.

Closer to home, now that Bree was off the hook, the rest of us could try to put the pieces of our lives back together.

First and foremost, that meant me figuring out whether I could stay with Finn despite the fact that he and Bree had had a fling. Despite the fact that he had a child with my cousin and best friend. Despite everything.

To give myself the space to think, I'd passed up home and the A-la-mode in favor of a red vinyl booth, a basket of onion rings, and a giant chocolate-dipped cone of soft serve. I'm not sure how Wayne found me at the Tasty-Swirl, but he did. I guess after seventeen years of marriage, we knew each other pretty well.

"Mind if I join you?"

"It's a free country," I grumbled. I licked a drip of melting ice cream as it escaped the edge of the waxy chocolate shell.

Wayne set down a tray loaded with two cheeseburgers and a basket of fries and slid into the other side of the booth.

I nodded toward the food. "What happened to your diet?"

He patted his rounded belly affectionately. "Well, I did try to keep eating right in honor of Brittanie, but I was having a lot of stress after her death. I tried taking up running, but that didn't take. Finally had to decide between maintaining my sobriety and my waistline. Sobriety won."

After our divorce, I learned that my husband suffered from a sexual addiction. I didn't begin to understand it, wasn't even sure I believed in such a thing, but I knew he'd worked real hard to get his life back in control. If he needed to binge on nachos in order to keep Little Wayne corralled, so be it.

He dunked a fry in a paper cup of ketchup and popped it in his mouth. "I heard about your troubles."

Good Lord. It hadn't even been twenty-four hours

since Char had been arrested. I pitched the half-finished cone in the empty onion ring basket and swiveled in my seat to dump them both in the trash.

"How is that even possible?" I wondered.

"Bad news travels fast in a small town."

"Huh. Then how'd it take me nearly two decades to find out you were cheating on me with everything in a skirt?"

Wayne winced as though he'd been burned, and I instantly felt chagrined.

"Aw, jeez. I'm sorry, Wayne."

He waved off my apology. "It's okay. You're right. I managed to cover my tracks pretty good. And there's something about you that makes people protective. I think folks kept hush because they didn't want to see you hurt."

I laughed. "Guess that fad has passed."

Wayne was tapping the excess ketchup from another fry, but he set it back in the basket, folded his arms on the table, and leaned in. "Tally, no one wanted to hurt you here."

"But they did."

"Yessir, I guess they did. But both Finn and Bree love you. Bree's the one that called me, actually. Said I should come find you."

"She called *you*?"

Wayne shrugged. "She was my sister-in-law for seventeen years. And she knows I want what's best for you. Same as she does."

I snorted.

"Tally," he chided, "they did the decd eighteen years ago. Eighteen years. What's the point in getting mad at them now for something they did way back then?"

I frowned at Wayne. He was right, dang it. The hurt was fresh and raw, but the injury was old. Real old.

"They slept together years ago," I said, "but every day since they've made a choice to keep it secret."

Wayne laughed. "Choice? You call that a choice? When exactly was Bree gonna tell you she slept with Finn? While we were on our honeymoon? Maybe when Sonny started courting her? After Alice was born? What would have been the point except to cause you pain?"

"Fair enough," I conceded, "but what about Finn? He should have told me before we started dating again."

"Really? Did you tell him about every shameful thing you ever did before you started seeing him again?"

I felt a bubble of impotent rage rising in my throat. "Why are you taking their side, Wayne? Why are you even here?"

He sighed. "I can't help but think some of this is my fault. I burned you pretty bad, and I think maybe you're taking it out on Finn."

"You're here to defend Finn?"

He dipped his chin and looked up at me with a "you know better" sort of look. "I'm here to do right by you, Tally. I can't undo what I did, the hurt I caused you. But I don't want to see you hurt now."

"It's not really in your power to stop it."

"No. It's not. It's in your power."

"Are you kidding? They're the ones—"

"They did what they did. But it's up to you how you react."

I sat there, stunned, staring at my good ol' boy ex. I couldn't quite believe Wayne Jones was capable of spouting such pearls of wisdom.

He must have guessed my thoughts, because he turned redder than a hothouse tomato. "That's something they teach us in Sex Addicts Anonymous. The only thing you can control is yourself."

I reached across the table and laid a hand over his. "I just don't think it's that easy."

"I didn't say it was easy, Tally. But does Finn make you happy?"

I pulled my hand back. "He did."

He nodded, as if I'd settled something for him. "Then you have to get past this. You can't let pride rob you of happiness."

Pride. Dang, I knew I wasn't proud.

I was scared. Finn Harper could crush my heart with one wayward glance. I didn't know if I could let a man—who was only too human—have that kind of power over me.

I looked out the window at the picnic tables across the parking lot. I'd been sitting on one of those very tables the night Finn Harper drove out of my life. He'd offered me his love, and I'd turned him down. At the time, I'd told him I couldn't run off with him because I had to take care of my mama.

That was true. But it wasn't the truth.

I'd said no to Finn because I was afraid of the unknown. Afraid to trust in something as insubstantial as love. Because I was desperate for the ordinary, the familiar, the secure.

Over the years, I came to realize those were foolish reasons to let go of love. I'd told Kyle that inertia was a poor reason to stay with someone. Turns out, it was a poor reason to lose someone, too.

Here I was again, back in the Tasty-Swirl parking lot, with a decision to make. Would I let Finn Harper slip out of my life again? Or, this time, would I close my eyes and leap into the abyss, trusting that he would catch me?

By the time I got home, Finn was sitting on my front stoop, right where I'd seen him the autumn before when he'd finally come back to Dalliance. He sat with his elbows resting on his knees, head in his hands, staring at the cement between his feet.

"Hey, Finn."

His head jerked up at the sound of my voice, and even in the fading light of day, I could see the hope in his eyes.

"I got your message," he said.

I settled onto the stoop next to him, tucking the skirt of my sundress around my knees. I felt sixteen.

"I've been thinking," I said.

"Uh-huh."

"Life's complicated."

A short laugh escaped him. "Amen."

"I like to color inside the lines."

"I know."

"But the lines keep moving."

He sighed. "I know."

I swallowed hard. "I think I need to learn to just be happy with the color. Worry a little less about the lines."

He laughed again, more softly. "You want to explain that for me?"

I shook my head. I wasn't sure I could put the idea into words that made more sense than that. So I tried a different approach.

"I've been thinking a lot today about Kristen. I never did figure out where she was from, find her family."

"I talked to Cal about that. He's going to see if the Dalliance PD can track down her people."

"Thanks." I grabbed his hand, knotted my fingers with his. "But I guess my point is that Kristen became someone else. She was a stripper and a lawyer."

"Sounds like the plot for one of those TV movies on the women's networks."

"Hush. I'm serious. You can't ever erase your past, but you shouldn't necessarily be judged by it."

"Thank you."

I shook my head. "Don't thank me. I'm not doing you a favor. I'm doing this for me. Bree and Alice and Peachy, they're my family, but so are you. Y'all are the colors in my world, and I couldn't give you up any more than I could give up blue. Or pink. I don't care if you fit in the lines, Finn. I just need you to fit in my life.

"I love you."

My heart pounding, I squeezed his hand.

And he squeezed back.

# Ice Cream Terrine
## with Deep Dark Fudge Sauce

With just a little advanced planning, you can turn store-bought ice cream into a pretty, company-worthy dessert. This is a mix-and-match recipe: choose any three flavors of ice cream, any (or no) tasty tidbits for between the layers, and any flavoring for the fudge sauce. A few yummy suggestions from Tally's ice cream imaginings follow.

*3 pints ice cream*

*1–1½ c. candy or nuts (pecans, peanuts, almonds, toffee pieces, crushed hard candy, crumbled peanut brittle, etc.)*

**FUDGE SAUCE**

*1½ c. heavy cream*

*⅔ c. brown sugar*

*½ stick (4 Tbs.) butter*

*4 oz. good bittersweet chocolate, chopped*

*3 oz. unsweetened chocolate, chopped*

*1½ tsp. flavor extract or 3 Tbs. flavored liqueur*

For the terrine: Soften the ice creams by allowing them to sit in the refrigerator for about 20 minutes. Line a 9 x 5 loaf pan with parchment paper, so the paper overlaps all four edges. Spoon ice cream, one flavor at a time, in the pan, using the back of a kitchen spoon or an ice cream spade and creating reasonably even layers. Sprinkle nuts or candies between the first and second layers of ice cream. Remember that the layer on the bottom of the pan will be on the top when you unmold the terrine.

Return the loaf pan to the freezer for at least 30 minutes.

For the fudge sauce: Bring cream and sugar to boil over medium to medium-high heat, whisking occasionally. Boil, whisking until the sugar dissolves. Remove from heat and whisk in butter, then chocolates, and finally the extract or liqueur.

To serve: Remove the terrine from the freezer. Use the overhanging parchment paper to unmold the terrine onto a serving plate. Slice and serve topped with a generous drizzle of the fudge sauce.

*Serves 6–8*

# Flavor Combination Suggestions

### Mocha Caramel Latte
*Ice Creams: chocolate, caramel, coffee*

*Nuts/Candy: toffee pieces (or crushed lady fingers, for frozen tiramisu)*

*Sauce Flavoring: coffee liqueur*

### Spumoni Special
*Ice Creams: chocolate, cherry (or vanilla), pistachio*

*Nuts/Candy: chopped frozen cherries*

*Sauce Flavoring: almond extract or almond liqueur*

### Banana Split
*Ice Creams: banana, vanilla, strawberry*

*Nuts/Candy: chopped unsalted peanuts*

*Sauce Flavoring: vanilla extract*

### Bananas Foster
*Ice Creams: banana, caramel, vanilla*

*Nuts/Candy: crushed peanut brittle*

*Sauce Flavoring: rum*

### Frozen Candy Cane
*Ice Creams: chocolate, vanilla, chocolate (or white chocolate)*

*Nuts/Candy: crushed peppermint*

*Sauce Flavoring: peppermint extract or schnapps*

## **Almond Delight**

*Ice Creams: coconut, chocolate, coconut*

*Nuts/Candy: chopped almonds (and shredded/sweetened coconut, if you like)*

*Sauce Flavoring: almond extract*

Read on for a sneak peek at
*Ice Scream, You Scream,*
the first book in Wendy Lyn Watson's
Mystery à la Mode series.
Available from Obsidian.

From the day I could hold a crayon in my chubby little hands, I have colored inside the lines.

I *yes, ma'am*ed and *no, sir*red and *pardon me'*ed. I smiled the right smile at all the right people. I dated the right boys and never let any of them get past second base until the day I married the right man. I shoved every last mean or petty impulse down deep into the darkest recesses of my soul, until I was as perfectly perfect as I could possibly be.

Yet still somehow I found myself up to my armpits in a vat of toasted praline pecan, scooping sundaes for my perfectly smug ex-husband and his perfectly bodacious girlfriend.

Proving beyond a shadow of a doubt that life just ain't fair.

"What kind of topping you want on that, Wayne? We got salted caramel, brown sugar pineapple, bitter-sweet fudge, and brandied cherries, all homemade."

Wayne Jones, my two-timing rat-bastard of an ex, hooked his left thumb through a belt loop on his Dockers and draped his right arm over the shoulder of the living Barbie doll at his side.

"What do you think, Brittanie?"

Because of course the little love muffin was a Brittanie. What else could she possibly be?

Brittanie heaved a sigh that sent her gazongas bouncing. "I don't know." She skimmed her coral-tipped fingers over her nonexistent hips. "I hardly ever eat sweets."

Wayne's lips curled. "Well, Tally is an expert on sweets. Why, I bet she's tried every possible combination. So why don't we let her decide?" He patted Brittanie's perky little butt. "What do you recommend, Tally?"

*I recommend you kiss my ample be-hind.*

Honestly, if the entire staff of Remember the A-la-mode hadn't been watching the exchange with eyes as big as low-hanging moons, if my biggest display freezer didn't need a new motor, if we'd had more than two paying customers that Saturday afternoon, and if Wayne wasn't thinking about hiring me to provide dessert for the annual employee picnic at Wayne's Weed and Seed . . . well, if it hadn't been for all that, I would have told Wayne and Little Miss Fancy Britches exactly what I recommended.

As it was, I bit the inside of my lip and counted to eleven in my head—counting to ten was never quite enough with Wayne—before plastering a bland smile on my face.

"With the praline pecan, I would go with the bittersweet fudge. The caramel would be redundant, you're allergic to the pineapple, and the cherry would just be gross."

"All righty, then. Let's give that a go."

I dragged my scoop through the luscious French pot ice cream that would put Remember the A-la-mode on the map, filled the pressed-glass sundae dish with two perfect globes of praline pecan, then ladled warm fudge sauce from the dipping well. With a slow, sensuous slide, the chocolate oozed down the sides of the scoops, forming a puddle of melted ice cream and fudge in the base of the glass dish.

Hand to God, there's something downright sexual about ice-cream sundaes, about the creamy, melty decadence of them. I felt like a pervert handing that sundae across the counter to my ex and his new girlfriend. Like I was handing them a sex toy or something.

I kept reminding myself how much money—and publicity—I could finagle out of the Weed and Seed employee picnic.

Outside of Texas, folks may not think of lawn care as a big deal, or a company picnic as a society affair. But the residents of Dalliance, Texas, take their grass seriously, and they're fighting a never-ending battle with nature to keep it green and free of nut grass and fire ants.

And while Wayne may have been a crap husband, he was a savvy businessman. He'd turned Wayne's

Weed and Seed into the CNN of Dalliance; the distinc-
tive lime green trucks were always plastered with birthday and anniversary wishes, announcements about the
latest Rotary event, and admonishments to support the
troops and get right with Jesus. In just under two decades, Wayne had parlayed a couple of riding mowers
and a Leaf Hog into a Dalliance institution.

When Wayne's employees and his best customers
got together to celebrate victory over another scorching Texas summer, the *Dalliance News-Letter* would be
there to record the event. Having my ice cream dished
up to all those people would mark an important step
in my transformation from Tallulah Jones, Woman
Scorned, to Tallulah Jones, Successful Entrepreneur.

Fingers crossed.

Wayne spooned up a big glob of ice cream and
sucked it in. Wayne's sweet tooth rivaled my own, so I
was eager to know what he thought. "Damn, Tally. That's
some fine ice cream. What do you think, sugar?"

I almost responded. After all, I'd been Wayne's
"sugar" for most of my adult life. But I caught myself
just in time as Wayne handed the spoon to Brittanie.

She dipped the tip of the spoon into the ice cream
and held it to her lips. She shuddered. "Ooh, it's way
too rich for me."

Wayne rolled his eyes. "Ah, geez, Brit. Lighten up
and have just a bite."

Brittanie thinned her glossy lips and narrowed her
deep blue eyes. In a heartbeat, the curvy coed went
from looking like butter wouldn't melt in her mouth to

looking meaner than a skillet full of rattlesnakes. I dang near got whiplash watching the transformation.

"I would think you'd be happy if I didn't pig out on ice cream, Wayne. I mean, you don't want *me* to get fat, do you?"

Whoa. Low blow. Behind me, I heard the synchronized gasps of Alice, Kyle, and Bree.

Apparently I was going to have to learn to count to twelve with Miss Fancy Britches Brittanie.

Wayne had the good grace to look abashed. He clicked his tongue against his teeth. "Dang it, Brit. Don't be a sore winner."

*Winner? Winner?* I couldn't count high enough to let that one slide.

"Lord a-mighty, Wayne, do you really think you're some kinda prize? I hate to bust your bubble, but I washed your BVDs for over fifteen years, and you ain't a prize."

That drew muffled snorts of laughter from the peanut gallery.

Needless to say, Wayne was not amused.

He flushed a shade of red I've only ever seen on baboon butts and the faces of self-important middle-aged men. A sort of precoronary crimson.

"Now, dammit, Tally—"

"Oh, hush, Wayne," Brittanie snapped. "You had that coming."

Wayne's lips thinned and a vein in his temple popped out. His eyes slid back and forth between me and Brittanie, and I could see the tiny wheels turning as he tried to decide who had pissed him off more, me or the twinkie.

I wanted to kick myself. With every pulse of that vein in Wayne's forehead, I saw my chances of catering the Weed and Seed picnic growing smaller.

Thankfully, Wayne decided the twinkie was the larger thorn in his side.

"Jesus, Brit," he growled. "You forget who butters your bread, little girl?"

Brittanie stroked the pendant at her throat—a delicate gold trio of Greek letters stacked one atop another—before tucking her arm through his and leaning toward him. She tipped her head down and looked up through mile-long lashes.

I'd seen this dance a hundred times. *Done* this dance a hundred times: the Ego-Strokin' Two-Step.

"Don't be angry, baby," she cooed. "Let's just sign that ol' contract with Tally and get ourselves home."

Wayne grunted assent. A wave of conflicting emotions overwhelmed me, leaving me light-headed and a little queasy. Gratitude and relief that, with Brittanie's help, I would get my contract. Shame that I had to sign the dang thing after Wayne and Brittanie walked all over my dignity. Revulsion at the thought of Wayne and Brittanie having make-up sex within the next thirty minutes or so.

Some images, a woman shouldn't have to endure.

Bree, Alice, and Kyle were still lurking behind me. I shot them a dirty look, and my niece, Alice—chronologically the youngest, but the most mature by a mile—herded her nemesis-slash–major crush, Kyle, and her mom, Bree, into the back room. I ushered Wayne and Brittanie to a wrought-iron café table and spread out my preprinted contracts.

"I've already filled in most of the details," I said, trying to sound efficient instead of desperate. "You tell me what you want and for how many people, and I can give you a quote."

Wayne made a big production of shuffling through the papers, drawing a pair of dime-store reading glasses out of his shirt's breast pocket so he could read through the fine print on the contract.

I sat quietly until he slipped the glasses back in his pocket and pushed the stack of documents toward me. He folded his arms across his chest, the big man back in charge.

"Looks fine, Tally. Are you sure you can pull this off on such short notice? We usually have a couple hundred people." He coughed. "But I guess you know that."

Awkward.

"So what would you like to serve?" I asked.

Wayne rolled his eyes. "Brittanie decided we should do a—a whatcha call it?"

"A luau," Brittanie supplied.

"Right, a luau. Pig roast and flower necklaces and stuff."

While I shuddered to think what kind of poi you could get in North Texas, and I'm not usually a fan of theme parties, a luau at least had the potential to be classy.

"All right; then maybe something tropical? Everyone loves Tahitian vanilla ice cream, and we could top it with fresh pineapple, mango, and a gingered cara-mel sauce. How does that sound?" Wayne frowned, but before he could open his mouth, I added, "I'll do some without pineapple for you, Wayne."

Wayne shot a glance at Brittanie. Out of the corner of my eye, I saw her give a tiny nod.

"That sounds fine, Tally. But here's the thing. I want to put the Weed and Seed stamp on this hoedown. So I'd like the ice cream to be green."

"Green?"

"Yep. Wayne's Weed and Seed green."

Wayne's Weed and Seed green wasn't just green, but an intense chartreuse.

So much for classy.

"Wayne, I don't know. I'm not sure how to get all that ice cream a real bright green without it tasting funny." I held my breath, praying he would just let it go.

"Well, how about that sauce stuff? Could you make that green?"

"I don't know. That's a pretty tall order."

Brittanie leaned forward in her seat and drummed a manicured index finger on the top of the contract. "I hear what you're saying, Tally. I really do."

Oh, lordy. It was one thing if she wanted to manage Wayne, but I wasn't too pleased at Little Miss Fancy Britches managing *me*.

"But branding is really important for a growing busi-ness," she continued.

I turned to Wayne. He shrugged. "Brittanie just got her degree in marketing from Dickerson."

"Branding," Brittanie said, giving the word as much weight as a bottle blonde with big ta-tas could. "We need the green."

She rested her hand on Wayne's forearm. "Baby, I know you wanted to help Tally out, but I think we should go with the original plan and have bright green fondant-covered cupcakes. I was so disappointed when Petite Gateau canceled on us, but I bet Deena Silver could help us find someone else. Lord knows we're paying her enough to cater the meal; she ought to throw in the dessert for free."

I bristled at the notion of Wayne throwing me a bone, giving me the job out of pity. But the ominously erratic hum of the display freezer was a constant reminder that I was in debt up to my eyeballs. I needed this job badly, even if it meant working with Wayne and Brittanie. Even if it meant making Day-Glo green sundaes.

"I can do it," I blurted.

Brittanie sighed and shook her head. "Really, I don't think—"

"No, I'm serious. I can do it. I can use a coconut sauce instead of caramel. I'll tint the coconut sauce green and with the fresh pineapple mixed in, the effect w be Wayne's Weed and Seed green."

Brittanie pouted, but Wayne reached for the tract. "Get me a pen so we can sign this thing."

I looked over at my display freezer, filled with of ice cream—rosewater pistachio, raspberry m pone, peanut butter fudge. My own recipes, m my own hands, in custom-made vertical batch

I'd designed myself. If I couldn't pay the bills and those freezers went kaput, my heart would melt right along with the banana caramel chip.

They say if you lie down with dogs, you'll get up with fleas. As I clicked my ballpoint and reached for the sheaf of contracts, I tried to pretend I didn't feel an itch coming on.